GW00363530

DEATH OF A DREAM

I thought of all the times Jacques had had his way by relying on moods and pouting and behavior far more childish than my own. I laughed a little, because it was that or cry over the dream that had just ended.

"Darling, I really am curious about one thing: why the odd figure? Why is it always six hundred thousand?"

That rocked him. Surely a gigolo knows he is a gigolo? But maybe they consider themselves superior to other men who lease out their sexual prowess because their stud fees are higher.

"You ought to see your face, Jacques. But don't worry. You'll be paid. I think you overcharge for your services, though. You aren't really *that* good in bed!"

His eyes glistened with insane rage . . .

The Richest Girl in the World

VIRGINIA COFFMAN

SEVERN
SH
HOUSE

This title first published in Great Britain 1988 by
SEVERN HOUSE PUBLISHERS LTD of
40–42 William IV Street, London WC2N 4DF

British Library Cataloguing in Publication Data
Coffman, Virginia
The richest girl in the world.
I. Title
813'.54 [F]   PS3553.O415
ISBN 0–7278–1540–7

66 120164 7 10456

Printed and bound in Great Britain

ONE/

WHEN I was just under sixteen and ran away to marry Jacques Levescu, one of Aunty's amusing young international acquaintances, I heard again the silly label the press had pinned on me: "The Richest Girl in the World."

I remember saying to Jacques, who was reading the paragraph aloud with a great deal of pleasure, "How can I be the richest girl in the world when my allowance is twenty dollars a week? Even Cook's granddaughter told me she gets more than that."

My devastatingly handsome bridegroom of nearly three days found this hilarious. He sat down on the scrambled sheets of the unmade motel bed and pulled me onto his lap. Marriage, at my age, was a license to discover at first hand, so to speak, the practical aspects of sex, and every time Jacques manhandled me, pulling me here, lifting me there, carefully curling his fingers over some erogenous patch of my anatomy, I felt that my own hot, pulse-pounding excitement was the real dividend of marriage. I was, of course, very young!

5

"Now, *ma petite*," Jacques lectured me that afternoon in his sensuous accent, pretending to bite my ear while his hands wandered over my inner thighs, "Let us, with great care, discover why they make lies about you, these men who write the columns of gossip. Is it that they lie deliberately? I think not. They know the vast financial empire of your respected aunt whom I am proud to call friend."

Secretly, I wondered if Aunty would be as anxious to call him "friend" after she found out about our runaway marriage, which was so like something my divorced mother might do, but I was engrossed in his reasoning, although uneasy at the responsibility of such much financial power.

"They are aware she guards it for you. And your grandparents had great power in many countries of the Western World. I happen to know also that your dead father, he too controlled great companies. All these go to you one day, my precious, richest wife in the world."

One thing about Jacques. He was naturally handy with figures. He explained all about my fortune that afternoon long ago, as a bright, gaudy sunset cut between the venetian blinds, striped the floor and fell across our bronzed and unclothed bodies. We had been making love earlier in the afternoon. "It's so decadent," I remember thinking. Now, he was ready for a pre-cocktail dip in Monterey's chill, invigorating surf, and there I was, sixteen year old Kay Amberley, as I look back on it, wildly immature, even when I freed myself to get into my black and white diamond patterned maillot bathing suit with its absurdly overpadded breasts. They only accentuated what probably were my skinny arms and my bony ribcage.

"You mean, some day I'll have to look at all those checkbooks and company reports and those trust account sheets Aunty gets every month from the bank?

That's terrible! People pay business managers lots of money to do that."

"My precious," Jacques reminded me whimsically, "I hope you are going to let me give you relief of those so-boring masculine problems. In my country such things are never handled by our females who are much too feminine. I shall be your business manager. Without salary; that is understood."

I wanted to tell him at once that I wouldn't insult him that way. "Oh, I wouldn't offend you by offering a salary, Jacques . . . I mean—darling." It still embarrassed me, this getting used to endearments. I had been reared in an atmosphere of cool, matter-of-fact and mutual trust, after my mother left my father. Mother had been almost over-demonstrative. I wouldn't dream of showing elaborate affection to my great-aunt Grace, any more than to my trusted girlfriends and boyfriends in the San Francisco public high school to which Aunty had sent me, over Mother's long-distance objections. We felt inside the family that our personal feelings were so strong, it was never necessary to resort to phony "darling" or "sweetheart" or even the ubiquitous "sweetie."

Of course, Jacques, my new husband—how thrilling that sounded!—was the exception. When he called me all those extravagent things, that was just his European custom. Anybody could tell he meant these wonderful words.

"You are so understanding, my sweet," he murmured now as he kissed me deep between my shoulder blades. "And you will be certain to tell *tante* Grace of my decision, that I will take no salary for my work in your behalf."

I assured him, conscientiously, that I would.

"And you realize that our living expenses will be most considerably above your twenty dollars a week. So that was an absurd little joke of yours, you understand."

It didn't quite penetrate for a few seconds. Then I

7

shifted, trying to move far enough away so I could study him.

"You mean—but we can't live on my allowance! I couldn't even live on it alone!"

"Well, hardly!" He laughed, showing his spectacular white teeth. "Is that what you thought I meant? Have you so little faith in me? I will attend to these things. I am the man. You must not question financial affairs again, my sweet. They are not the province of the female. So?"

My nearly sixteen-year old heart thumped so hard against my bathing suit that I was ashamed for him to see it and guess how thrilling, how indispensable I found him, the only man in the world who treated me as a delicate and very feminine . . . female!

"We'd better go for our swim, Jacques—"

"Sweetheart."

"Y-yes."

"Well then, you must say it."

"Sweetheart." It sounded funny when I said it. Insincere. The way actors said it in a play. But Jacques seemed satisfied and when he had grabbed up our terry cloth robes, we hurried out across the early California-style motel grounds to the path down the cliff. The cove was below, and already the long Pacific waves rolled up the beach and back, leaving in their wake a stretch of wet sand that gleamed with golden flecks in the sunset light.

"Look, gold. Everywhere. Exactly like your fortune, My Richest Girl in the World!" Jacques pointed out as we ran together along the sand.

I wished he would not talk about my money, or remind me of the silly title. It made me feel oddly inferior. I told him so, as I tried, breathlessly, to keep up with him.

"Don't call me that. Please. I wish you wouldn't."

8

He squeezed me hard around the waist, and then pulled me to him.

"*Trés bien, ma petite.* But I assure you," he added, for emphasis, "I promise you, your fortune does not change you in my eyes. I love you fully as much—No. Better—than if you were poor as—" He grinned. "Poor as I."

"Thank you. Thank you, my husband." I still lacked more than an inch of my present height; so I stood tall and kissed him on the mouth before he expected me to. For an instant his full lips were cold, then he warmed to me, jokingly called me his "Precious Heiress" and I reached down, grabbed a handful of sand and pelted him with it.

After that, he chased me into the surf and we had a wet, merry time of it. It wasn't until we got back to the beach and lay down briefly before returning to the motel grounds, that I began to worry about wiring Mother in Hawaii, and especially Aunty at home.

"She'll kill me. She'll be so mad."

Jacques pretended to look terrified.

"What? Is she so dangerous? You promised not to worry until the week was gone."

"I know. But I wish we could at least tell her where we are."

"Darling, you exaggerate. Madame Grace has always been kind to me." His eyebrows arced gracefully. "Most kind. . . . At times, almost too kind."

I stared at him. I didn't quite understand my own prickling of resentment at this insinuation.

"Not Aunty! I can't believe it. Why, she's old enough to be your mother."

He shrugged, turned his head in the sand which flicked over my cheek and I was impressed again by the incredible fact that a man of Jacques Levescu's enormous

9

charm and good looks should choose to marry an inexperienced, gauche young woman like me, who didn't even have her own money to handle.

I said something of this to him that afternoon and though the ocean breeze was rapidly chilling our bodies as well as the sand, Jacques warmed me by his smile as he pinched my nose, and then said quite seriously, "Do you know, I believe you may be a great beauty one day. It is of considerable help that you are blonde. Much can be done."

"Much can be done?" I was ridiculously hurt. I had grown up in the shadow of a mother whose beauty was almost a legend, and whose attention to that beauty was far greater than her attention to her child. Only a few days ago Jacques and I were driving down the Peninsula on our way to get married and he told me "his lovely Kay Amberley was the prettiest girl in town." I didn't believe it. I wasn't *that* young. But I had thought he found me attractive enough the way I was, so he wouldn't have to make me over. Not quite yet, at least.

"Sweetheart, you are trembling. We mustn't let our bride take pneumonia less than a week up from Mexico. What will everyone think? That your new master takes very bad care of you."

I didn't like to think of Tijuana and our quick, unromantic wedding. I let him fuss over me, putting his arm around my shoulder to "keep you warm. . . . You need a fur. You know that? A girl of your station in life."

I thought that was funny at a moment like this. "A fur on the beach?" My shivering had stopped with his touch, but as we climbed the cliff to the back gate of the motel, his idea struck me funny. I think it annoyed him that I laughed.

"Not on the beach, silly child. But for every day. For dinners when we return. That sort of thing."

"I have a mink stole Aunty used to wear," I suggested

doubtfully. "She had it made over for me. But she thought I was too young to wear it except for special. I didn't even wear it this spring when I graduated from high school."

His frown made me uneasy. I had come to dread it and watch for it, trying to swerve off to another subject, something that would please him whenever I saw that frown.

"Jacques! What is it? Did I say something wrong? Oh, darling, don't be mad. I'll wear the ratty old thing if it means that much to you."

"You need not. You need not please me. I do not wish to establish myself as a dictator in your life. That is," he added, yielding to my efforts, "unless it is for your own sweet sake, child. Then—*then* I am adamant. Remember, I am your master always. But only for your benefit."

I agreed eagerly.

"I know. And I want you to be my master. It sounds so—" I looked at him with my heart in my eyes. "It sounds so romantic. . . . Master!" It titillated me to be someone's slave, especially to be enslaved to a man so exciting, so handsome in my sixteen-year old eyes.

"That's my good girl." He patted me on top of the head. The gesture spoiled my mood, seemed to me just a tiny bit patronizing. But after all, I remembered, he was twice my age. I must seem childish to him at times. I would have to grow up, or at least mature, rapidly, to keep up with Jacques.

More and more though, I found myself wanting to call up my great-aunt Grace and tell her where we were, that we were on our way back home to San Francisco, having driven up El Camino Real from the Mexican border. I was never really afraid of Aunt Grace's anger, only of her disapproval. She had a way of being sardonic, witty and just plain sarcastic, which was her method of punishment, and I often wished instead, that she would haul off and give me a big, hard smack on the rear when I deserved

11

punishment. It would not have made me feel nearly as bad as her witty and usually wise remarks.

"What are you counting, my precious?" asked Jacques when we were returning to our motel from the surprisingly good roadside restaurant on a bluff that overlooked foggy Monterey Bay. "Are you counting your millions?"

"Don't!" Then, hurriedly, I corrected my abrupt and angry tone. "No, I mean—please don't. Actually, I was counting the days before we'll be home to take our medicine from Aunty like good soldiers."

"I see." The rather soft line of his chin and lower cheek was shadowed as he stared out over the dark Bay with its distant flickers of light, like tiny gleams from a toy Christmas tree. "Kay, my dear, you must stop referring to your great-aunt as if she were still your guardian. She should not be. I am your guardian now, and I must have your cooperation, your trust. . . . And above all, your insistence that I replace your aunt in the management of your affairs. As is proper in a good and faithful wife."

"But Jacques, Aunty has always handled things. I just couldn't try and turn her out of my life like that. She's been a regular mother to me."

"How quickly my little slave rebels against her loving master!"

As I tried to explain, he removed his arm from around my waist, very slowly, with a kind of emphasis. "Please, I do not wish to know more of your real feelings tonight. I have been deceived. That is all."

"No, no! I never deceived you. I've always told you how I feel."

"You led me to believe I was first in your heart. How can I care for you, become truly your loving master when you shut me out? You put an old woman—a female—before me!"

I knew when he took that tone things were critical,

12

and I tried to explain, before he went into one of his strained, long-suffering silences that both hurt and frightened me, because afterward there was coldness, "a mood" which kept him from touching me again that night. And I lay there for hours in the big motel bed, near Jacques' stiff, unrelenting body, but not next to it. He seemed far away. I felt terribly cold and lonesome and scared. I even wondered if I had done wrong, acted too hastily, in running away to marry the hero of all my movies, all my dreams, everything a fifteen-going-on-sixteen-year-old girl could ask for.

A dozen times in the cool night I wanted to creep over and touch his sleek, bare flesh, dark against the white sheets, but one thing kept me from making the gesture. It seemed like a betrayal of Aunt Grace. And even for Jacques, I couldn't do that.

I cried a little, silently, wiping my eyes on the sheet, and trying hard to keep from sniffing. Jacques always got frightfully annoyed when he caught me sniffing. He said it made him nervous and it spoiled his "lovely image" of me.

In the morning, though, everything became different. The weather was briskly sunny and salty, with blue skies, and I felt encouraged. My small world would be happy again.

It was all rather odd, the way it worked out and Jacques' mood changed, or at least, it seemed so at the time.

I remember that after a few hours' sleep, I woke up suddenly. Jacques seemed to be still sleeping, lying on his side, his back to me, very stiff and uncompromising, his face half-concealed by the pillow. But I could see his dark, slightly thinning hair with its wiry texture that I liked to crinkle between my fingers when he would let me. Jacques always put slathers of oil on his hair, some European habit, I thought. Once, I had made a joke

13

about "greasy kid stuff" but he didn't think it was funny, and I hadn't dared make any suggestions about his grooming again.

I got up and showered with a mere drizzle of spray, because I didn't want to wake up Jacques before he was ready. He might go on sulking. . . . No! Not sulking. That was for babies. Moody. He was just artistic and moody. I slipped on my prettiest yellow satin bra and panties, and his favorite buttercup yellow sheath, a style that was all the "bit" that year. I pinked-up my normally pale face with a blusher, silvered up my lips and sneaked into the bedroom barefoot, on tiptoe, so as not to disturb Jacques unduly.

I was re-doing my hair, brushing it out in long, firm glossy strands, and trying to figure out what style would make me look older, more sophisticated, when Jacques' strong, lean fingers slipped around my neck, under my hair. They had just begun to massage my throat muscles in the sexy way he knew so well when my brush accidentally hit his knuckles. He pulled his hand away, wincing, as I dropped the brush and cried, "Oh, darling—darling, I'm so sorry! I didn't mean to. Honestly. Does it hurt?"

He laughed. While I was in the bathroom, he had gotten up and put on the quilted red and black satin dressing gown which made him look like a youngish Rumanian man of distinction, but very sexy, too.

"My darling slave, you did not come to me in the night and beg pardon for your mistrust. Nevertheless, I forgive you. You win. Let us be great friends with our revered Madame Grace. You will tell her of your treatment by your husband, how he protected you, married you immediately. No panky-hank—"

"Hanky-panky." It made me laugh but I was careful not to let him think I was laughing at him. Even then, I must have known, subconsciously, that most handsome men have no humor about themselves. "Jacques, could

14

we drive right on up to San Francisco and see Aunty today? And start our normal life. Our married life."

"Why not?" He lifted me off the floor, holding me under the arms and pinching my breasts in a way that made me cry out. "My little slave's slightest wish is the command of her loving master. . . . Remember, sweetheart, that you are a woman now. You must live quite differently from the poor little girl of high school who could not even wear a fur coat. You must impress this upon Madame Grace."

I sighed with contentment. How thoughtful of me he was! My pleasure, my happiness, he was so insistent upon them! I knew Aunty would understand that.

TWO/

AUNTY UNDERSTOOD. I sometimes think, looking back on it, that she understood things and people almost too well. I began to call her "X-Ray Eyes" when I was old enough to sass her back. I wasn't quite old enough that day when Jacques and I drove up to the old house in Pacific Heights, one of my hometown's innumerable hills, and parked on the steep side street so Aunty wouldn't see us drive up and be prepared for us in her marvelous, theatrical way.

"You have to curb the wheels . . . turn them in toward the curb," I explained and then, seeing Jacques' face harden a little, I tried to make a feeble joke out of the remark. "Otherwise, we'll roll right down to the Bay."

"Do not advise me upon my driving, ma petite. It is most unfeminine. Come now. Remember! Your loving master will stand between you and any punishment, any harshness of Madame Grace. Do not be afraid."

As he demonstrated by drawing me close to him,

16

close to the exciting warmth of his body, I confided happily, "I'm not afraid. Honestly. A little nervous, I guess, but I'm so anxious to see Aunty, and show you off, I just haven't time to be scared. After all, the worst that can happen is that we will just go off and live our own lives until I am eighteen and get my own money. Nobody can touch us, now that we are married."

I thought this would relieve him of one worry, at any rate, but it didn't seem to. Inconceivable as it might be, I suspected my sophisticated and worldly new husband was more nervous over meeting Aunty than I was. This made me secretly very protective of Jacques' honor and his "face." The way Japanese people talked of the importance of "face." Well, it would be my turn to protect Jacques from Aunty's biting tongue. We would get a head start, by arriving unexpectedly.

After breakfast, we had driven up from Monterey, and if we were lucky, we would be invited to lunch with her. Unless, of course, it was her yogurt day!

I noticed that we were walking awfully fast up the hill to our street but decided it must be because Jacques was as anxious to see Aunty as I was. The big, square house looked almost strange to me since my marriage. Seeing it through Jacques' continental and elegant eyes—he had never been more than a brief visitor at formal affairs —I saw all sorts of flaws. The house's patterned brick façade looked so old-fashioned I resented it, all of a sudden. The trim was only one brick deep, I had been told, as Aunty went through the 1906 earthquake and fire and was definitely allergic to brick as a building material.

It was apparently not our home's old-fashioned look that bothered Jacques entirely, although I didn't think he liked it. I saw him looking over the rear of the house which was built down the steep hill on one side, two narrow floors, progressively narrower as they descended the hill.

"I suppose those are your quarters for the servants."
I almost laughed but luckily didn't.

"Not on your life! You couldn't get a servant to live below Broadway, the street on the front up there. A play-room is on the bottom floor. Down there. And one of Aunty's rooms. A kind of library-study. Next above is a —I guess you'd call it a ballroom. You were there the night of my graduation party when the European Chari-ties met with Aunty at the same time. My own bedroom is a cute little one on the third floor, on the back. It has a low, slanting roof on one side, a what-you-may-call-it, and it makes me think I'm in Paris. I get a staggering view out of my big, slanting window. Just like an artist. Only mine's a view of San Francisco and the Bay. I love it."

He rolled his eyes skyward as if my naïvéte was be-yond his comprehension. And it probably was!

"That shall be remedied. Does it occur to you, My Sweet, how shockingly inappropriate it is that the owner of all this wealth should be shunted away to a tiny attic room, while others, mere caretakers of the fortune, should occupy the fine suites, the best rooms?"

"But it's not true! Aunty is my guardian. She has al-ways handled money. Since she was a girl."

We were passing the front of the house now and I lowered my voice, hoping he would do the same, be-cause one of the long windows in Aunty's modernized Victorian parlor was open and Aunty often sat there working on her endless account books, because it was so comfortable and warm there, in our chilly climate.

Instead of ringing the door bell as anyone else would have done, Jacques carefully raised the big brass knocker and let go while I shuddered, imagining the reverbera-tions throughout the lower floor and up the heavy, com-fortable old walnut staircase just behind the foyer. . . . "The hall" as most of us called it. When Jacques had

18

visited the house earlier in the month, it was always in a group, at a gathering of Aunty's various charity heads, that sort of thing. And there was a formal dinner, or a tea where everyone balanced eggshell tea cups on knobby knees and concentrated so hard on not breaking the china that Aunty got her way for any plans she might have.

I realized then that Jacques would expect to see the butler Aunty employed on formal occasions, but Hildy opened the door for us. Hildy had started out as kitchen help when Aunty was first married, and by hard work, persistence, and a crazy, scratchy kind of charm, she made herself indispensable to us all. She stood there now, her thin, dry features faintly bored, and her harsh voice said, "Well, don't stand out there all day. Fog's coming in and you two'll freeze in those sexy clothes."

Jacques looked as if he might resent this familiarity. Besides, he was not any more sexily dressed than a turtle-necked white sweater, slacks and huaraches could make him. But I hugged Hildy and kept saying incredulously, "You aren't surprised. You aren't the least bit surprised."

Inside the house I tried to introduce Jacques to Hildy as she hurried us along, but it was uphill work. Jacques was upset over something, probably Hildy's manners, or lack of them, and Hildy, unfortunately, never concealed her opinions of anything. Her opinion of my husband was summed up in her brisk, "All right. He's the guy. I'd know him a mile away. Your Aunt Grace is waiting in the red parlor. Chin up, kid." This to me. "You aren't dead, yet."

There was a brief second or two as we walked into the Red Parlor when I almost wished I was dead, or at least somewhere else. Anywhere. My great-aunt Grace was sitting in her maple rocking chair with its tomato-red pads that fought with the crimson plush of the other chairs and the sofa in the room. However, the long windows facing south and west caught any sunlight available, and the red furnishings gave the room a cozy warmth even on the most foggy day. Aunty had her stocking feet up on a worn, plush-covered hassock, and a dime store notebook, fastened to a clipboard, balanced on her knees. I think Jacques was surprised at how goodlooking her legs were in their sheer nylons, because he stared at them, speechless, for a minute while I ran toward her, then stopped abruptly, waiting, rather like an over-friendly pup, for that pat on the head that would allow me to throw my arms around her.

She was in her early sixties then but seemed ancient to me, and venerable as a Buddha. In later years, as I grew more mature, she seemed much younger. She had a small, round face and was always pretty, with her short, curly gray hair and her youngish, deceptively vulnerable-looking mouth. Her blue eyes might have frightened as well as they enchanted a great many men. But one look at them now, even though they were partly framed by Aunty's sardonic eyebrows, and I went right into her arms. She dropped the notebook with which she had been comparing a Trust Account statement from the Wells Fargo Bank, and hugged me.

"Well, Katy, so you went and did it! And now you expect me to eat you alive!"

I felt a tiny bit uncomfortable because my cheek was suddenly damp with Aunty's tears and Aunty was not a woman to cry easily. However, she gave an angry sniff and turned off the few tears with her usual determination. She pushed me away a foot or two and, still holding me by the shoulders, studied me.

"So you really think you are a grownup married woman of fifteen! A baby like you!"

"Sixteen, Aunty. Next week I'll be sixteen. Don't forget."

Jacques interrupted here in his nicest voice. I often thought it sounded the way satin feels when you run it through your fingers: soft, shiny, with funny little unexpected barbs.

"I intend to devote my life to your niece's happiness, her comfort and pleasure, Madame. I give you my *parole*. That is to say, my word of honor."

Aunty let me go slowly and looked at him, and I began to be uneasy. Everything had seemed so simple, so friendly when she hugged me, and studied me with her wonderful, all-seeing eyes. But with hardly a muscle changed, she now looked up at my husband exactly as if he were a fly she was thinking of swatting. I didn't see how she could have shown such a kind, good, loving face to me and seem so different a second or two later, without a great change of expression.

"Oh yes, of course. Your . . . honor. That will be of great help, Mr. Levescu. Your honor." It was amazing how she made that nice word sound like an obscenity, and Jacques turned red as sunburn.

"I assure you, Madame, my honor, the Levescu honor, means more to me than my life. However little the subject may be worth to . . . others." It was a splendid speech. I almost applauded. It brought back to me wonderful memories of my first movies, when Errol Flynn made speeches exactly like that. My mother would love Jacques when she finally met him.

"Bravo. Bravo," said Aunty who evidently was also reminded of those dear old movies. She smiled and her mouth looked warm and inviting. It was too bad the smile didn't move upward where the tiny wrinkles at the corners of her eyes still showed signs of her recent tears, and her eyes were more flinty than I ever remembered. Much as I loved her, I thought she was being too hard on poor Jacques just because he was poor. After all, he

21

came from a very distinguished and ancient family. He had confessed that to me with what I thought was a really touching mixture of humility and pride.

Hildy stuck her head in the doorway.

"I put their junk in your Paw's room, Miss Gee, like you said. Cook says lunch any time."

I could see that this news perked up Jacques no end, but it seemed a bit overwhelming to me. Great-Grandfather's room was enormous and stuffy, with whole walls of books, and a big brass bed that always made me think of dead people because we had gathered around that bed after Great-Grandfather's last heart attack.

"No, Aunty! That isn't fair. I have my own room and I like it a lot better. Really!"

Before Aunty could say anything, Jacques pulled one of the red plush padded chairs away from the wall and though he hadn't been asked, he sat down on it beside Aunty. It made him look very much the master of the house, and I was surprised by a sudden, pinching resentment at his usurpation of a place that didn't belong to him yet.

"Madame Grace is quite correct, my precious child. You must accustom yourself to taking your proper place in the great world."

"Good Lord!" said Aunty with a wry smile. *"My Precious Child!* Now, I've heard everything. Next, your husband will be calling himself your slave."

"Oh, no," I started to explain. "It's just the reverse, actually. I'm his—"

"Madame Grace," my husband cut in so fast he was almost rude. "If we may retire now and make ourselves presentable to appear before you at lunch?"

Aunty kept on smiling, a little broader. "By all means." As we got up to leave, she asked Jacques, "Did you see many movies when you were a boy?"

Jacques looked both puzzled and wary.

"Yes, Madame. Why do you ask?"

"I just wondered if your dialogue came naturally, or if it was a carryover from your Saturday matinees."

THREE/

THERE WAS a ghastly silence. Ghastly for me, at least. I felt like sinking through the heavily carpeted floor as I shared, or thought I shared my husband's humiliation. He seemed to recover with an admirable rapidity, however.

"I was reared in Paris," he said with hurt dignity. "We did not have what you call Saturday matinees." He added with his exquisite politeness, "If you will pardon us now?"

I felt sure this was the best poor Jacques could do on the spur of the moment, and I suffered for him when I heard Aunty's brief spurt of sardonic laughter the minute we left the room. Still, I felt that she accepted our marriage. She would surely be nice from here on, as long as Jacques behaved in his charming way. Above all, I didn't want Aunty to think I was a "love 'em and divorce 'em woman" like mother.

And then, I could see I had Jacques to contend with too. His body was so stiff as we walked up the wide, worn old staircase, that I could hardly get a grip on him. I took his chilly hand. He started to turn left in the big second floor hall.

"No, honey. To the right," I corrected him.

24

"Always the little helper, always right," he sneered, deliberately using my words as a weapon against me. I was absolutely crushed, of course, at these, his first sharp words to me, but while we walked into Great-Grandfather's big bedroom suite, I reasoned away my husband's sharpness. After all, he had been under terrific strain trying to out-maneuver Aunt Grace verbally. He probably didn't realize that no one had ever done that, so far.

The minute we were inside Grandfather's bedroom, however, I didn't have to worry about my husband's mood. He was pleased. He rubbed his hands, exactly as if he had been freezing cold and now was warm. Leaving me in the doorway, he walked around the room, giving a kind of brief touch at the elegant, heavy—and I was sorry to realize—dusty old furniture, mostly mahogany. He loved it.

While I was thinking that there might be difficulties ahead between us, since he always loved regal old things, and I had such plebeian modern tastes, he finally sat down on the big bed, testing the springs, and held out his hand to me. He was smiling, that beautiful, forgiving smile which was the prelude for his return to good nature. And no one could have been more relieved than I to see it. In those days my happiness was solely bound up in others' moods. In this, as in other ways, my life subsequently became almost the reverse. One learns from experience. And above all, I learned from Aunt Grace.

"Well, *ma petite*, this is something like. The richness! The luxury! It suits you; don't you agree?" He was running the gold fringe of the bedspread through the fingers of his free hand as he spoke.

I looked around and found everything both depressing and sickening and almost said so. It was terribly hard to hold in my personal feelings and opinions like this.

25

"There, there. . . . Do not look so depressed, *chèrie*. I have forgiven you; don't you see?"

"Forgiven *me*?" I echoed, wondering if I had heard him right.

He hugged me to him, stifling my face against what Hildy called his sexy sweater. I was relieved in spite of my secret disagreement with him. I reasoned that he was older than I. His taste might be superior, even though it seemed garish and guided always by the monetary worth of the object. That might be the standard of things where he came from.

I said meekly, "Thank you, sweetheart," but for the first time, I felt the hypocrisy of my agreement.

"My loving little slave," he murmured. "And she deserves to be loved. Now, this minute."

I wasn't really in the mood, and was secretly relieved when Hildy knocked with her usual brisk authority and asked if there was anything we needed. Jacques couldn't possibly know about the towels in Grandfather's bathroom, but for some reason I couldn't fathom at that moment, he called out in a tone I felt was almost arrogant, "Yes. You may have more towelling robes brought. And send one of your house girls to wait on my wife until I can choose someone appropriate."

I heard something like a gasp and then Hildy's shrill voice, "How's that again?" She pushed the door open and stuck her head in. "Did I hear right?"

Jacques pointed to her tousled head and snapped his fingers. "Never open that door without permission. You understand me?"

I cleared my throat, tried to smooth things down, but Hildy had the last word: "Oh, don't you worry, Mr. Levescu. I understand you, real well! I want a little talk with you, Kay, when you're ready. Alone!" The door slammed.

"It's a good thing the door jambs are solid," I remarked, wanting to laugh hysterically.

Jacques lips locked hard together, making him look surprisingly old. Then he managed to control himself. "That woman is intolerable. This is what comes of giving females control of a great fortune. No true elegance. Permissiveness among servants and other inferiors. A waste of your money in corporations that collapse, and trusts that are mere bits of paper."

I looked surprised, and a little apprehensive, and he smiled tenderly.

"I want many things for my precious child . . . furnishings worthy of her, clothing, furs that do justice to her position. And cars. Motor cars. That dreadful old Cadillac of your Aunt's. . . . Really!"

"But she doesn't go out that much. And I'm not quite old enough, she says."

"You are now. Or at least, I will drive your car—when the chauffeur is not wanted. And I will choose the cars for you. A little sports model, I think. And a large, comfortable Rolls. That will give the chauffeur a bit of work, keeping it properly. And then, if we oust your aunt from this position she has snatched, and which she fills so badly—"

"But we can't! I love her. She's been good to me."

"Naturally, my little slave will pension the woman. See that she is always cared for. Your generosity is one of your most endearing qualities. No one knows better than I on our honeymoon, what your generosity meant to us. And I will be behind you always, guiding your steps." He kissed me carefully and fully upon the lips, his tongue very busy in my mouth.

I simply wasn't ready for a soul kiss when I was worried about explaining away Jacques' continental manner to Hildy and wondering if Jacques really, way down

27

deep, thought he could handle the Amberly Estate better than Aunty. I thought of Aunty, as long as I could remember her, with her dime store notebooks carefully ruled in columns with a pencil, and every cent of sales tax noted, every two-cent chocolate peppermint I used to take at the cashier's counter after a restaurant lunch, and of course, every dime spent on a newspaper, every fifteen cents spent on a cable car into Union Square for shopping. Maybe Jacques wouldn't fuss with such small items. He would be too busy buying us new Rolls Royces and yachts and lovely glamor stocks. Even at not-quite-sixteen, I instinctively felt that Aunty's way was more secure. Less fun, but more secure!

However, I was too afraid of my husband's moods and smouldering angers, to tell him what I really felt. I kept thinking: "I'll let him find out gradually. In that way he'll get used to the manner in which we live." I also thought of asking Aunty and Hildy to be easy with Jacques and maybe to pretend to go along. I made up my mind to speak to Aunty about this as soon as possible. But not in Jacques' hearing, of course.

As it turned out, the hardest task I set myself was to speak to Aunt Grace alone. My new husband flattered me by preferring that I never be out of his sight. It got to be a little tiresome after a while, though we did get through lunch pleasantly enough. Jacques and Aunty only disagreed once in my presence. I felt sure Jacques was trying terribly hard to be at his agreeable and charming best.

On our way down to lunch Jacques suggested as he squeezed my hand possessively, "Perhaps it is better if we do not tell the good Madame Grace our little secret . . . What we are to each other."

I didn't get it for a minute. "What we are?"

"I am your master. You are my slave."

"Oh, that!"

28

"It would be better to keep that our secret. Our small love secret; isn't it so?"

Yes. Aunty certainly would have something sarcastic to say over that. I nodded my agreement and we went in to the sunny little breakfast room where Aunt Grace and I usually ate when we were alone. Jacques didn't like it. I could see that. But he was very nice about it. He only looked around a couple of times with a contempt that was quickly concealed. Everything in the old-fashioned but pleasant room looked shabby as I saw it for the first time with an elegant stranger's eyes.

Jacques and Aunty spent most of the nice plebeian lunch—a tuna casserole of all things!—going over plans for one of the Amberley charities that had tentacles of a nicer sort, reaching into Iron Curtain countries. This was the subject that first brought Jacques to our house, and while they were busy discussing the one subject they had in common, I wondered for the first time how much truth there was in my husband's hint that Aunt Grace went for him. She seemed quite friendly toward him at that moment, so much so that I ventured to interrupt their discussion.

"Aunty, why wasn't Hildy surprised when we popped in here today? Did you know we were coming?"

She smiled that little patronizing smile which never offended me, because there was always justification for it. She had out-smarted someone. "My dear girl, an hour after you managed to get rid of your virginal state the legal way, I knew all about it. I've had days to get over my—surprise."

"Who told you? We didn't see a soul in Tijuana that we knew."

"Well, thank heaven there' was someone who knew of you at the hotel where you had dinner. A friend of mind and his wife. One of those race drivers. He'd just won the Grand Prix at that track near Mexico City."

It needled me just a little when Jacques said with sudden enthusiasm, "So that is who he was! I thought I recognized Sebastiani across the dining room. Had I known he was a friend of yours, Madame, I would have introduced myself. . . . And my wife," he added a trifle belatedly. "He is a brave man, this Sebastiani. The women adore him."

"You mean you saw Sebastiani and didn't notice Claire, his wife?" Aunty asked Jacques. She turned to me. "Gorgeous creature. Sickly, or so she pretends. But gorgeous. One of those French Blondes. I detest her, myself."

We all laughed, but Aunty hadn't yet settled my curiosity.

"But how did you guess we'd be home today?"

I should have known we couldn't get ahead of Aunt Grace.

"It being too late to save you from—" She glanced at Jacques and then away, "—from disaster, I simply had you followed up the Coast. I'm told the weather was delightful at San Clemente, though a bit foggy at Monterey. We all more or less expected you back yesterday. But apparently you found amusement enough to keep you at Monterey last night."

Jacques and I exchanged glances. I was embarrassed, and I was fairly sure my husband shared my feeling as we remembered the *amusement* that kept us at Monterey.

But Aunty only smiled grimly and repeated a cliché that my grandfather, her brother, used to say a lot: "You have to get up pretty early in the morning to out-fox me, my girl." Like a great many clichés, it happened to be true. At least, it was true of Aunt Grace. Jacques seemed to want to test his own acumen against hers because, before I could ask to see her alone. . . . "to straighten out a few matters," I was going to put it, my husband, with

30

great formality, asked if he might have a private conference with her.

"Without your wife's presence?" Aunty asked, making the most of the omission.

"Let us say," he began smoothly, "I wish to speak of so many lovely things about my little girl that she would be utterly spoiled if she heard them."

Aunty persisted with her jabs, "You talk of my grandniece as your little girl. Yet it would be a trifle awkward to attempt an annulment on grounds of her age, in view of—ah—Monterey and Tijuana and San Clemente. In fact, rather than a little girl, I am led to believe she is very much a married woman."

"Quite true. Very true!" Jacques agreed with haste. "As you say, we are married, beyond any doubt, in the eyes of God."

"Don't bring God into this, Levescu. God washed His hands of you long ago." It was humiliating to me to hear the tone she used with him and the way she called him so abruptly by his last name. It was even worse, the way he answered her, with his biggest smile and an ingratiating manner I couldn't help thinking of as insincere. But maybe he felt this was the best way to get her on our side. I could have told him different.

As soon as I politely could, I made a silly remark like: "Don't mind me!" or "I'll leave, so you can talk about me," and got out of the room. I bumped into Hildy in the hall and tried to apologize for Jacques' foreign manner, which had been so offensive to Aunty and my old friend.

Hildy hustled me through the Music Room which used to be the Sewing Room when I was a child. Aunty loathed sewing and had taken a sudden, fleeting taste for playing the harp, ten years ago; so now, though nobody touched either the harp or the old treadle sewing machine, the white and gold oval room was pretentiously called "The Music Room." I must remember to tell Jacques about it. It ought to impress him. When we were definitely out of hearing of Aunty and Jacques, Hildy reassured me in her abrupt, hearty way, "Don't be silly, Kid. I got that bird's number. You needn't worry about me taking him seriously. We'll get you out of it in no time flat."

"But I don't want to get out of it, Hildy! I've never felt this way about any other man. And I never will again."

Hildy sputtered with laughter. "At sixteen, the girl says this! Wait'll you've lived a little, Kay."

It was this kind of "You're so young" talk that made me more anxious than ever to make a go of my marriage. Everyone always failed in marriage. Even my mother and father married just to unite a couple of dozen corporations. Or so I'd heard people hint. Heaven knows, Mother had done the same thing all over again, though now her taste ran more to good looking gigolos. And I had figured out by the time I was fifteen and a half that the secret was: women didn't look up to their husbands. They didn't idolize them and become lovingly enslaved to them. If I did that, I simply couldn't fail. I would be Mrs. Levescu until I died at some ancient age and on my tombstone would simply have to be carved: "She was a perfect wife."

"Anyway," I told Hildy proudly, "I know the secret of happy marriage."

"You do! Well, what is it, Miss Know It All?"

"You just do whatever your husband tells you. Then he can't say there's anything wrong with you."

"Oh, brother!" With that, Hildy left me at the stairs and I went up absent-mindedly all the way to the third floor and my pre-Levescu bedroom.

I realized my mistake the minute I opened my door, but

32

I looked in anyway, trying to tell myself Jacques was right. Great-Grandfather's suite was much more comfortable. Or if not more comfortable, more beautiful. No! Not even that. The more I looked at my little attic room with its friendly, comfortable window seat and its fabulous view of three-quarters of San Francisco Bay, the more I began to wonder at my husband's taste.

Maybe I could get Aunty to forbid us to stay in that stupid, ugly room of Grandfather's. And she might forbid us to do some of the other odd, extravagant things Jacques had in mind. It was cowardly of me, but expedient.

Meanwhile, what on earth were Aunty and my husband thrashing out that took so long? I was dying to know, but on the other hand, I didn't want to be caught sneaking around listening. To kill time, and because I knew Hildy and Aunt Grace would make me do it sooner or later, I got all my clothes out of my third floor closets and threw them on the bed, complete with hangers. Then I loaded on my arm enough outfits, hangers and all, so that I staggered as I trotted down the hall to the narrow, back staircase we used to call "the Servants Stairs" before our democratic autocrat, Aunt Grace, took over the Amberley Home Place.

Chiye, a quiet, terribly pretty Japanese girl that Hildy was training for service, met me on the stairs. I know I was much more flustered than she was. In fact, Chiye gave me an inferiority complex, with her bland, and to me, expressionless face, her easy grace in the cute, full-skirted white uniform Hildy had, surprisingly, designed for women in Amberley service. Hildy's own long-waisted, shapeless black dresses, holdovers, I thought, from the Flapper Twenties, always showed stains of some sort, but she was positively scrupulous about starchy cleanliness in others, including me.

"Help you, M'em?" said Chiye, looking shy, though I felt instinctively that she knew me far better than I knew her.

"Thanks. You could, if you're not too busy, help me unload my clothes from my upstairs bedroom to the big one on the second floor."

Chiye hesitated.

"I do not know if I am expected below. M'em Hildy says always 'do not dawdle.'" She looked as though she might refuse me, which was the sort of thing I always ran into. Out of politeness, I suppose, she had suggested she could help me. But on being challenged, all her helpfulness petered out. Jacques was right. I ought to learn to handle my own affairs. Stop letting Aunt Grace and Hildy do all the work. I had begun to learn that the giving of orders was more difficult than the taking of them. The only thing was, I instinctively felt that my husband's Old World way, treating servants as serfs, was no more correct than my own hesitancy with them. I said to Chiye, hating myself for the propitiating smile I gave her, "That's all right. Don't bother. I'll do it."

She stared at me out of her beautiful, expressionless dark eyes, and did not smile back.

"If you wish, M'em." She went on past me.

Feeling stupid over what I considered my excessive and humiliating friendliness, I dragged my clothes down to Great-Grandfather's suite where, as I hung them on the rickety rod in one of the closets, I found myself thinking that I didn't really want to do this at all. I wanted to live upstairs in my own white attic bedroom with its window seat to curl up in on a foggy day, and read an Agatha Christie while I ate raw pine nuts and peeked out now and then to see if the Golden Gate Bridge Towers were still floating above the fog.

But when I glanced around the big mahogany and brass bedroom and saw Jacques' elegant clothes, already

34

unpacked and hung neatly in the opposite closet, I got the now-familiar excitement at the pit of my stomach and thought of the hours of delight he had shown me on that odd, vagabond honeymoon trip up El Camino Real from the Border, and said to myself, "You're lucky, Kay Amberley. It isn't every girl who gets a master like Jacques Levescu for her sixteenth birthday."

Really, he and Aunt Grace had been chewing me out quite long enough! I put off bringing down the rest of my clothes and favorite possessions until I could find out what had happened between my two "masters". It was rather funny, I thought, while I hurried downstairs two at a time, to think that they were arguing my life, my future, with my money, and without my opinion on anything. I wondered, just as a game, a kind of mental exercise, how I myself would handle my life, but in the short time I gave myself to solve it, I couldn't seem to come up with any ideas that Jacques and Aunty wouldn't handle better.

Still, it would be fun, and excellent experience, if I could try.

Aunt Grace's voice was surprisingly loud, for Aunty. She didn't sound angry, only businesslike, as she spoke to my husband in the Breakfast Room, with the door ajar.

"You rate yourself very highly. What precisely are the contributions that make you so valuable? I must tell you, I examine all purchases that are brought into this house. My grand-niece brought you in. You say you are worth something over half a million dollars. For six hundred thousand dollars I always expect a big return on my investment. Do I make myself clear?"

. . . . Oh, Jacques? I thought, clenching my fists and wincing for my poor husband who was being so cruelly insulted. . . . Hold up your head. Snap your fingers at her cynical offer, and I'll run into your arms and one

35

day make you so rich you'll be glad you couldn't be bought!

I took hold of the partly opened door and started to walk into the room, but I wasn't fast enough.

My husband's voice, even now, was beautifully pitched, carefully warm and it evoked memories of those marvelous nights of our honeymoon.

"Madame Grace, I do not boast. I am not dishonest. Nor am I humble—"

. . . Bravo, darling! I thought.

"—because I know my worth. You must realize that six hundred thousand dollars is merely a pittance. If I take my wife away from you, I take her immense fortune."

I held so tightly to the door knob that my fingers ached.

"Not for two years," said Aunty calmly.

"I can wait," said my husband.

My knees were shaking, but I managed to walk into the room. The two people who had been disposing of me looked around guiltily. I couldn't speak at first. There was a big, choking lump in my throat.

FOUR/

"PLAY DUMB," my heart and my brain told me during those numbing seconds. "Play dumb and everything will be just like it was. Pretend. That's all."

Aunt Grace recovered her voice first.

"Good heavens! You startled me, slipping up on us like that. What do you want, Katy?"

Jacques was perfectly calm, more calm that Aunty, but he stared at me with an odd, intent expression, as if trying to warn me of something.

Swallowing rapidly several times, I managed to laugh and say in a funny, light voice, "What do I want? I want my husband, of course. You two have been locked up in here for ages."

Jacques stepped over to me and hugged me to him. I was surprised at myself, how easily my body could thaw and pretend it was not emotionally stiff as a poker.

"My poor bride! You must remember, Madame Grace, we are still on our honeymoon, and it is a bad thing to attempt to separate honeymooners."

Aunt Grace looked from Jacques to me and then, as

she got up, she remarked in her dry way, "So I see. Well, run along, children. We will resume our little business discussion later, Levescu."

I said to Jacques when we left the breakfast room, "I wish she wouldn't keep calling you Levescu, darling. It isn't as if she doesn't know your name."

He patted my shoulder soothingly.

"A small matter. You know, my precious child, you handled that delicate moment in a very adult manner. I am proud of you."

I knew perfectly well that what I had heard was not a dream, and yet, kept repeating to myself that this whole scene hadn't happened at all. Any by the time we got up to Grandfather's suite, that dream part of me took over and assured me, Jacques was only going along with Aunty to draw her out.

"Congratulate me, *ma petite*," my husband said triumphantly when we were safe from being overheard, in Great-Grandfather's bedroom. He stood there proudly before me, with his hands on his hips, and one of his "good mood" expressions.

My secret trouble was so overwhelming I blinked and stared at him.

"C-congratulate you? How?"

"I told you I would see to your rights. You need no longer be a begging child at your aunt's feet. I've seen to it."

I began to see vaguely where this was leading. But because I wasn't sure of my own feelings, I said nervously, "Yes, yes. Go on."

He reached forward, clasped me to him. For the first time since he kissed me on the night I fell in love with him, I had no reaction. I felt his body, the bone and muscle and the flesh warm against mine, and yet they did nothing for me, aroused no emotions except an uneasy feeling that I wanted to be free. Just free for the moment. Undoubtedly, all his sensual power over me would return later when I could forget or shake off the scene I had walked into in the Breakfast Room.

He knew almost at once that his power over me had failed momentarily. He did not let me go. His arms felt surprisingly hard, like ropes binding me to him and I began to sense an inward panic of my own at my revulsion. I had married my husband without a religious ceremony, but it had never occurred to me even once that we would not be married forever. How could we fail? I was going to be his loving and well-loved slave. He could never find grounds for falling out of love with me.

It hadn't once seemed possible that I might fall out of love with him!

"Sweetheart, raise your head. Look at me. I know my precious child has something troubling her. Is it because of what you heard your Aunt say to me so rudely? And you minded. For my sake. But you mustn't. I can take care of the rude old lady." His hands crawled over my breasts, lingering on the sensitive zones so that, try as I might, I could not prevent the tell-tale erection of the flesh beneath his feathery playing. It was the old way that had always aroused me, but this time I panicked and cried out and tried to wriggle away from this stifling embrace. Reluctantly, and all too slowly to suit me, he let me go. I backed away, looking up at him immediately, trying to make my face appear as bland and expressionless as the face of Chiye Mitsushima.

"Jacques, it's wonderful if you out-maneuvered Aunty. How did you do it? Tell me while I put my clothes away."

His limpid eyes seemed to harden a little. He was watching me much too carefully.

"You call me Jacques now. So cold! No matter. I have planted the seed. With a trifle above half a million dollars we may live where and how we choose, until your eighteenth birthday when you will be. . . ." His eyes

39

lighted in the way that had been, until this minute, the promise of such magic minutes, such heretofore unknown physical pleasures. "My darling child, you will be mistress of the world then. And I. . . . ?" He prompted me in the way that had enchanted me on our honeymoon.

"And you will be my master," I murmured the way I had when asked to recite the Multiplication Tables. As his eyebrows arched I added nervously, "My adorable master."

"Ah, that is better." He leaned forward, kissed me so gently, so charmingly, on the forehead, that I felt the power of the man soothe and conquer me to my very vitals.

We said no more on the subject of his conversation with Aunt Grace while we went ahead with our unpacking. Later in the day, Aunty sent word by Hildy that she would talk with me about "my future plans" if I could see my way clear to do so that day. I would like to have discussed my problems, my doubts, my plans—if any— with someone. But, to tell the truth, I wasn't at all sure of my own feelings, or whether I really wanted to know the truth about my dashing, handsome husband, if it meant destruction of my happiness. Who could tell when I would know such happiness again? If ever. Aunt Grace would be sure to be right. She always was. And I thought: if I could just prolong my honeymoon for a little while! Prolong the exquisite physical sensations that Jacques had taught me on El Camino Real. . . .

And face the truth tomorrow. Or next week. Or even in a month.

And then followed the most damaging thought of all, the tiny, poisonous thought that came to me for perhaps the first time in my life and became my watchword, my hideous, comforting, eternal truth as I saw it, the words: *"But I can afford it."* I could afford to keep on being mar-

ried to Jacques Levescu, to re-live and re-experience the
sensuous pleasures he had taught me. I could afford it
as long as I chose.

But my pride would end it, of course.

It never stopped surprising me to watch the ease with
which Aunt Grace and my husband got along when they
were thrown together, during meals or passing in the
hall as Jacques and I were on our way to some of the fabulous restaurants of my hometown, though it always
looked odd to me when I was not served cocktails before
dinner. Jacques was careful about this, one of the little
"protective master" ways he had of making me feel more
feminine and younger than ever. I was flattered, and in
an odd sort of way, it titillated my senses so that I was far
more receptive to his greatest talent when we came home,
and I almost forget that we were making love in Great-
Grandfather's bed.

Although I hadn't asked for it, Aunt Grace gave us a
party which was really rather funny, because the guests
were evenly split between the Scotch-drinking, champagne cocktail group of men and women over eighteen
whose focus was my husband, and the rest of the guests
who were part of my high school gang. Our excitement
was furnished by Cokes, and a certain amount of natural
animal spirits. A couple of the kids brought flasks of
bourbon, which the rest of us tried to ignore. We hadn't
used the description "camp" yet, in those days, but we
knew the bourbon was less important to them than the
idea that they were re-living the Twenties hip flask bit,
and we resented their phoniness.

My best girl friend, Ann Forrester, tried awfully hard
to bridge the gap for me, between our school crowd clat-
tering around the "Ballroom" in a noisy Rock dance we
had created one dull Saturday night, and the very sophisticated group surrounding my husband.

Ann was a year older than I, and except for the drinking, managed to fit much better into both groups than I did. She was dark and quiet and not too exciting, and I began to mature that night when I realized I could learn a good deal about life and "fitting in" from a girl most of us had always liked but considered a bit out of things.

Even Jacques, I found, appreciated Ann's grownup and ladylike qualities. Late that night, as Suzie, an upstairs maid, was running his bath for him while eyeing my husband in his quilted lounging robe that was slightly parted, Jacques coaxed me over to where he sat half naked on the bed, and gave me some husbandly advice.

"As a married woman, sweetheart, you will have to choose your friends with a bit more care."

Nervous because I suspected he might be heading toward something I knew but wanted to deny, I pretended innocence.

"H-how do you mean?"

"My precious, I adore you as my child bride, but I did not marry the entire teen-aged world of San Francisco. Didn't you notice tonight how much more dignity and manners one found in the adults at your party?"

It was just what I expected, but I resented it all the same. "They didn't do me any good. They were all drinking, and I don't drink. Not in Aunty's house, anyway."

"*Your* house," he reminded me implacably. "And I think, when you consider very carefully the two groups tonight, you will agree that your wild young school friends do not belong in your husband's world."

Suzie stood there before us, grinning at Jacques.

"I hope the bath is the way you want it, Mister. . . . Sir."

I was happy to note that he ignored her attempt to flirt with him. His thoughts were obviously somewhere else. He got up to take his bath but stopped long enough to pat me embarrassingly over the groin, and make the smiling but quite serious comment, "You could do worse than observe your friend, the young lady you call 'Ann.' Her manners are very adult."

I didn't know why—it wasn't jealousy—but I secretly envied my best friend and made up my mind to study Ann, and maybe "mature" myself, not only to satisfy Jacques, but because the party that evening had taught me that he was right. I no longer felt myself one of my high school crowd.

During our first month at the old house on Pacific Heights, Aunt Grace suggested several times that she and I ought to have a "chat" about the future, but I always made excuses. I knew, or thought I knew, what she wanted to talk about, and judging by all my past experience with her, she would have mountains of proof if she wanted to convince me of what I already knew. She even dragged Ann Forrester into her conspiracy to explain about my husband's real motives. At least, I thought it was Aunty who was responsible for Ann's nervous telephone call one Tuesday morning at the time of University Signups across the Bay at Berkeley.

"Hi, Kay. Are you busy?"

It was one of those questions that are impossible for an adult to answer honestly without giving offense, but at our age, we understood the question quite well.

"No. What's up?"

"Are you alone?"

I looked around. I had answered the phone from the kitchen where I was trying to argue Cook into making mince meat turnovers, though I was the only one in the family who liked them.

"Speak freely, Ann. I'm alone."

Cook and Chiye Mitsushima who was on an errand for Aunty, plus Cook's friendly eleven-year old granddaughter, Julia, all raised their heads and looked at me with varying degrees of indignation. That is, Julia giggled, but the others were less amused and I whispered to them, "Sorry. No offense." Then I said into the phone, "What's it all about?"

"How are you fixed for lunch?"

"Terrible. Nothing I like is on the menu."

"Can you meet me somewhere for a sandwich or something? I've been over at Berkeley signing in all morning and I'm starved."

I asked her where she was now, but all the time I was convinced that she had something on her mind besides lunch. The trouble with Ann, I told myself, definitely not for the last time, was that she took everything so seriously.

"Suppose we meet you at the Franciscan on the Wharf. We can count the ships as they come under the Bridge."

We often did this, one of us choosing Incoming, the other Outgoing, and the one who counted the most ships in her direction was treated to lunch. That, of course, was when we couldn't get a boyfriend, a schoolmate, to pay. This time, though, I was sure there was more to it, and it angered me that she should try to add a nostalgic note to our meeting.

"You said 'we.' Jacques is down on Montgomery Street right now, studying some of my stock and bond portfolios. He has an idea for a few changes."

Ann said hurriedly, "No. I meant—I didn't mean that. See you in an hour. Okay?"

"Right." I had to change my tired, beat-up peddle-pushers for something fairly presentable, but I hurried through this and met Aunt Grace coming in just as I was leaving the house for the waiting cab.

"Where are you rushing to in such a hurry?" she wanted to know as she reached out, almost mechanically, to straighten the neckline of my bright, sunburst Hawaiian sheath. When I told her, she smiled. "Good girl. By the

44

way, that orange color doesn't do anything for your hair. Was it your husband's idea?"

I said rather crossly that it wasn't, "But I can't wear blue, green and lilac forever, you know. I get sick of it. And it's so immature."

"Well," she agreed to this with a sigh. "At your age, I suppose nothing looks bad on you."

I gave her a quick kiss that brushed her soft cheek, and rushed out to the taxi at the curb, thinking as I often had, that I'd like to have Aunty's skin when I was sixty. Nevertheless, I was sure she had put Ann Forrester up to this lunch invitation for reasons that threatened Jacques.

". . . . And I can't give him up yet," I admitted to myself as I climbed into the cab. I kept remembering the nights with him, the exciting "brief encounters" during the day, when we thought no one suspected. "I can't give him up for a little while. . . . After all, I can afford him for a while. . . ."

When I got to Fisherman's Wharf the morning fog was being pushed aside by one of our virulent winds and the sun thawed out the air, giving every object an ultra-sharp, glistening look. It invigorated me and brought back some of my optimism about Jacques. As I crossed to the wharf-side restaurant, which is shrouded in glass high over an expensive gift ship, I kept finding more and more to be said in favor of Jacques. Or, at least, in favor of what I had observed of my husband, during the weeks since the very mercenary discussion between him and Aunt Grace.

After I made up my mind that day, when I eavesdropped, I had been so careful never to bring up money or to question Jacques on how our expenditures were handled, that I had discouraged Jacques on the subject, as well. Maybe it was this reluctance of mine to bring up the subject that caused Jacques to sheer away from teasing me about that idiotic title "Richest Girl in the

45

World." Now, even when someone else brought it up at a party, he veered the conversation off the subject. Possibly, I thought, he has found out it isn't true. As for me, I didn't know whether it was or not, and didn't care too much, at that age.

I rushed up the stairs to the restaurant, was met by the maître d' and, as usual, shunted to a cluster of waiting, would-be diners. If only I had been a few years older, I could have waited in the cocktail lounge adjoining, where the picture window view, like that in the restaurant, displayed the stunning sight of the Golden Gate, the Bay and Alcatraz, carved in the windy sunlight. I was surprised when a tall, good-looking, rather intense man, maybe thirty, came up to me and started to take my arm.

"Miss Amberley? Ann has a table by the window. Shall we?" I thought at first that his accent was Southern, but it made me think of Western TV shows, though there was nothing of the easy drawl about it. I understood later, of course.

"I'm really Mrs. Levescu, you know," I reminded him. "Didn't Ann tell you?"

"I beg your pardon. Mrs. . . . Levescu." He said it as if he hated the name. I wondered if he knew Jacques. I hoped this wasn't Ann's surprise, her reason for inviting me to lunch, in order for this stranger to tell me a lot of lies, or unpleasant truths about my husband.

Ann was waiting for us in her quiet, friendly way, and something of her quietness always rubbed off on me, for the better, when we met.

"Hello, Kay. It was nice of you to come at such short notice."

I tried to guess, from her expression, whether she had something unpleasant to tell me . . . Damn all friends who can't keep their advice to themselves! . . . I thought. Ann's tall friend seated me by the window, opposite Ann, and then went around to sit beside her. He

46

was terribly proper and stiff; yet he had the odd, muscular quality that seemed not to suit the Proper Bostonian manners. Some of Aunt Grace's ultra-conservative friends in California and Arizona politics behaved with this curious ambivalence. Aunt Grace had friends in every camp, most of them violent. She could needle any side of any subject, and often did.

"Kay, meet Morgan Haight. He's south-western director of Daddy's merchandise market. He's—" She smiled, a rather shy smile, and blushed a little. "He's terribly nice. Morgan is from Texas."

"I figured that," I said, flatly and deliberately turning to the waiter who was offering me a menu. The size of the menu momentarily hid my face from Ann and Mr. Haight, during which time I tried to figure out what Mr. Haight had to do with this emergency meeting. Jacques had already taught me to look to him, not the waiter, when I ordered, and I glanced at Morgan Haight now. "Whatever I have," I told him, "I want the potatoes with it. They're sort of scalloped. Only better here. I adore them."

Mr. Haight's gray eyes examined me. His smile was cold. I could almost see his thought processes at work. I was much more juvenile than his friend Ann. She wouldn't be caught dead "adoring" scalloped potatoes. Maybe he was right, at that. She probably felt about his teaching as I felt, up to now, about Jacques' careful cultivation of whatever good manners I had acquired but not yet used.

"Do you think—Shall I have a seafood salad?" Ann asked her friend and as I watched her, I saw that her normally calm brown eyes were almost glazed with what must be adoration. It gave me a jolt. I adored Jacques, but for very physical reasons. It was a little frightening to see that, out of nowhere, Ann felt even more violently over the cold-eyed man.

47

Had I really sounded so slavish when I ordered meals through Jacques? The sight of this girl, so much less volatile than I, acting even more enslaved, shook me. Quite suddenly, I saw myself as Aunt Grace and Hildy and my school friends must have seen me when I returned from my honeymoon. And again I heard Jacques' smooth voice enticing me to call him "master." I remembered how he had remained indifferent to me in bed, rousing my senses, my nerves, then pausing, with the insidious whisper: "Call me your master. Say you are my slave. My slave . . . Say it!" And then I had whispered it, with my knees shaking, my loins on fire, and we made love.

But I had thought we were special, that the things he taught me, the many variations, the 'sodomy' were daring, enjoyed only by highly sexed people, as I thought of myself during those days and nights of my honeymoon. And after. In Aunty's house. Good Lord! In Great-Grandfather's bed! Did he know? How shocked he would be!

Ann saw me staring at them, and she said softly, "A lot's happened since you ran away with Mr. Levescu to Tijuana. Morgan came up from Dallas for the Conference, and he's been wonderful to me. I'm growing up . . . I really am. Aren't I, Morgan?"

He passed his lean hand over hers but did not prolong the touch. His expression was sober. Grave.

"If Ann matures as I have every reason to believe she will," he said to me, "and if she graduates from the University with a B average or better, we intend to marry shortly after."

"After four long years?" I bellowed. People at surrounding tables bobbed their head up. I didn't mind them, but Mr. Morgan Haight's expression chilled me to the marrow. He turned to Ann.

"Ann's father agrees with me that Ann should not ven-

48

ture into anything so solemn without a great deal of preparation."

I wondered what sort of preparation he had in mind that would take four years, unless, of course, he really cared that much about Ann's receiving a diploma. But before I could say anything stupid about that, he went on.

"We haven't discussed the—ah—problem with Miss Amberley yet."

Ann looked scared. I would too, I thought, engaged to be engaged to this monolith.

"Not, but—that is, could we eat first?"

This was a pleasant start! I had been about to correct him again as to my married name but I was now anxious to get to the point.

"What's this all about, Annie?"

"I'm afraid—I'm awfully afraid it's about your husband. About Mr. Levescu."

I wanted to scream: Oh, God damn it! No!

But I didn't, naturally. I raised my eyebrows, trying for Aunty's sardonic expression, and said with all my cool, "Well, what about Mr. Levescu?"

FIVE/

"KATY—" Ann reached across the table, but I got my fork in the way and she almost stabbed herself. She retracted the unbearably sympathetic hand and ventured with a quick glance at Morgan Haight, "I'm so sorry. But you see, Morgan's sister-in-law, Georgia, she's a widow."

"So?"

"Well, it seems that she fell in love with a slick, handsome—ah—"

"Gigolo?" I asked brightly.

She flushed, and Morgan cut in. "As a matter of fact, yes. He persuaded her to elope with him to Juarez where —Thank God!—she awoke to her disgusting mistake. It finally took over half a million dollars to buy him out of her life."

I felt hot all over, even the roots of my hair, the toes of my feet, as I managed, with enormous effort, to laugh.

"My Lord! Why do you say "over half a million"? Why not half a million? Or three-quarters?"

50

"You'll have to ask your friend Levescu about that," Morgan announced, shrugging. He turned to Ann. "You were right. The seafood is excellent."

Ann ignored him, for once.

"It's some fetish, Morgan thinks. The man—I mean your—Mr. Levescu demanded and eventually received six hundred thousand dollars. He became a dreadful nuisance before they paid him off."

Through my tangled, ugly thoughts one clear, vile truth cut its way: the six hundred thousand dollar figure was no coincidence and it proved the rest of the detestable Haight's story was quite real. And he picked some old silly widow. . . . He probably told her, on their way. to Juarez, that *she* was the prettiest girl he'd ever met. . . . He probably taught her a lot of wonderful—No! Loathesome things to do in bed, also. And all the time he was laughing at her as he must have laughed at me. Or worse. Suppose I disgusted him and every time he made me call him "Master" he shuddered with revulsion at the touch of my flesh . . .

"Katy, are you all right?"

"Of course, I'm all right. But did it ever occur to you wise characters that I find my husband worth it, for the present?"

"For the present?" Ann echoed, as if she couldn't believe what she heard. She turned to Morgan for help. "You must convince her. Tell her what a nasty creature he is. Why, he'll bleed her white!"

I didn't have to look at Morgan Haight's handsome rigid face to guess his contempt for me, the sixteen-year-old mother of all idiots! While he spoke, supporting Ann's plea, I didn't glance at him. I was looking out the window as a girl's voice at a microphone reported the name and flag of "Amberley freighter Mission Bell, American in from Hololulu, final port of destination, Los Angeles."

"You are very young, Miss Amberley, and you don't realize how expensive men like Levescu can be."

I flashed around, showing all my teeth in a huge smile as I said, too loudly, "*I can afford him.* As long as he amuses me. Up to now, he's been awfully amusing. And educational." I added to Ann, with pointed emphasis, "I doubt if you'll ever know how educational!"

Ann gasped, and even her Texas friend stiffened alarmingly. I got up, causing a panic among waiters rushing to help pull my chair back. I acted terribly scatterbrained and flighty.

"Look, kids, I know you want to be alone, and I'm really awfully hungry. Can we take up where we left off, some time soon? Gotta run."

And I did.

It was lucky I wasn't wearing high heels or I'd have taken a header down the stairs. I ran across the street, threading through the usual Fisherman's Wharf crowd of tourists and up past Sabella's corner. There was a trolley bus on Columbus Avenue that would, at least, head me homeward, though I'd have to transfer or get a cab at the end of the line, but then I'd be home. I couldn't bear that.

It was another block to the turntable of the Bay Street cable car. I hopped onto the car just as it was rattling back up toward distant Chinatown and the shopping district beyond. This made me laugh. How often I. Magnin's and Ransahoff's Fur Salon and the city of Paris had been Mother's refuge from unpleasantness at home! The thought of the shops didn't entice me now, though. I sat huddled into the corner where I was gradually pushed as the car clanged up the hill above Columbus Avenue, collecting a capacity crowd as usual. In my huddle of misery I tried to think what to do, but all I could come up with was the obvious fact that I had to be freed from Jacques, and I wasn't sure I wanted to be, in spite of

52

what I knew perfectly well must be the truth about him.

I kept appealing to my pride, because my senses obviously wanted to hold onto the pleasures and delights I had known. And my delight in being Jacques' "slave," guarded and protected by an older man, suggested to me now that another of my husband's enchantments was due to my need for a father.

Perhaps I worked too hard lashing up my pride, because it gradually began to impinge on my senses. By the time my mind was made up, I discovered the pleasures and pains of my sudden, youthful marriage had left marks upon me that I knew would remain for years to come.

"Love—sex and marriage based on them—are illusions," I told myself with the wisdom of my great experience. "They are weapons used by the unscrupulous. You must be ruthless to enjoy them. If a sensual partner has used your need of him to gain money or power or influence, just adopt his means to satisfy your own needs. But never, never give yourself, your feelings, emotions, without full knowledge that it will cost you."

On that sunny afternoon, the wind in its San Francisco way blew so hard it dried my tears of self-pity and lashed me into a fierce determination. By the time I jumped off the car at the St. Francis Hotel block and started across the Square to the big department stores, my mind was made up. I love strolling through the stores, though after the divorce between Father and Mother, I was always aware of the legend in our family that Mother's moral lapse had begun with her extravagance in San Francisco's delightful shops. The fact that most of these were department stores patronized by middle-class housewives in those years before the teen-age market took over, made them seem harmless as playthings for the very wealthy Myra Amberley. They hadn't been harmless, though. Mother ran up bills buying a fantastic collection

53

of items, clothing, jewelry, furs which she never wore and turned over in the most casual way, to servants and any friends or acquaintances who would take them. Her answer, when accused of extravagance, was that "there was plenty more money where that came from, and besides, she was bored."

At last, I knew how Mother had felt. At least, for "boredom" I would substitute "heartbreak." Except that buried deep in my thoughts, was the little prick of uncertainty. How could I be heartbroken when, from the very first, there had been a romantic, movie quality about Jacques' attraction to me? My mirror and my honest friends showed me I was a rather ordinary girl in those days before the cosmetic and coiffure industries created the miraculous beauty mask that anyone could acquire. But when Jacques raved about me, I had no 'Lolita' aura to attract a handsome, worldly, experienced man. I thought of all the women he had known, so many beauties. And some of them rich.

My world brightened momentarily. He had known beauties with money, so it must have been something else that had attracted him to me. After all, there were plenty of rich women.

But then I remembered how often he had repeated my idiotic title, "Richest Girl in the World." How he had savored it! And I remembered Morgan Haight's sister-in-law, and Juarez, and above all, that particular sum by which they had bought him off: six hundred thousand dollars. It was no use. He was a gigolo and he had never loved me.

I got sick all over again when I thought of the good times that lay between us in memory, and above everything, the feeling that I belonged to someone. Really belonged! I walked across to the City of Paris, a store whose French owner came around the Horn to success, like my Great-Grandfather. Usually, when I went in, I thought

54

of the store at Christmas, with its magic, sparkling decorations, but this time, I was glad it wasn't Christmas. I had dreamed of sharing the holiday season with the man who took care of me, was my master and guardian, the first man since Father's death years ago.

To keep from thinking, I started to buy. I bought trinkets. And then stationery and nylons and a bed jacket, though I'd rather be dead than wear one, and then I got into the Men's Shop and saw a quilted lounging outfit that would have looked so romantic on Jacques, and I felt so bad I went to the women's rest room and cried my head off, flushing the toilet frequently so people couldn't hear me crying.

On my way down to the street, looking pink and dishevelled in spite of my efforts with comb and lipstick, I saw a display of Hawaiian prints, complete with Waikiki Beach Sand, and outrigger and a palm tree. And I remembered how I had secretly pictured Jacques and me on the beach, or on our lanai, watching the gaudy, glorious sunset. It was too much. I was sniffing again, and Jacques hated to hear me sniff.

I ran out to the street and tried to hail a taxi, and when I got one after running more than a block and risking life and limb, I said to myself: Jacques was right about that, anyway. I need a car for myself, maybe two.

I believe now, with the perspective of time, that the girl I was that day, had grown up a little by the time she returned home in the afternoon. I saw someone's figure behind the old-fashioned crisp lace curtains of our suite, but I couldn't make out whether it was my husband or one of the servants. Hildy came to meet me at the door, though this was certainly not one of her duties.

"That man's been asking—demanding, I guess you'd say—to know where you've been. What's up, Kay?" She took my bundles of packages but wisely asked no questions about them.

I knew by this time who "that man" was, but I didn't feel like going into it now. I said tiredly, "I've got to see Aunt Grace. Is she still downstairs, or up dressing for dinner?" Aunty wasn't formal, but somehow, she always looked regal and stunning in whatever she changed to for dinner, even when only she and I might be present.

"Sure. She's tucked up like usual in the Red Parlor. Going to go up in a few minutes." As always, Hildy was ahead of me. "But you take your time, Kid. Anything you gotta say, that comes first with your Aunty."

I said hastily, "Thanks, Hildy. I'll explain later," and I took off for the Victorian Room and Aunt Grace who was unflappable, no matter what.

It is curious that I remember every little detail of our meeting, Aunty's and mine, that day, perhaps because it was one of those crucial times in our lives, or mine, at any rate. When I came into the Victorian Room with its heavy crimson padded chairs and its old-fashioned comfort, I felt at home as nowhere else. Contrary to my usual interview with her, Aunty wasn't sitting down, working out her figures on the day's, or the week's expenses. Aunt Grace was standing at one of the long windows, looking out at the street. Her precious pencil-ruled notebook was on the floor, the pages all bent up and bent down, terribly sloppy. Not like Aunty, at all. Yet she didn't look angry when I came in unexpectedly. Just tired and rather sad.

"Hi, Aunty," I greeted her, terribly bright and flip.

She said, "I wondered when you would be getting home. How is Ann Forrester?"

"Awful. She's in love with a fellow who'd scare his own mother."

"Morgan Haight. Yes. I know about him. Good man." I started to say something and she smiled faintly, ironically. "Well, that's the story I get. However, I'll admit he

56

sounds too good to be true. Where did you go after you left Ann on Fisherman's Wharf?"

I began to prickle up all over. "Aunty! You knew all along. Did you send me down to see them today? Couldn't you tell me yourself?"

She held out one small, imperative hand. "Come over and look out the window. Look down there."

I didn't want to, but I couldn't resist Aunt Grace's ancient hold over me.

"I don't see anything. Except that car parked there at the curb. Kharmann Ghia; isn't it? Is someone visiting us?"

She sighed and dropped the curtain down into place again. "This is not a Kharmann Ghia neighborhood. Your husband bought it for you. At least, he says it's for you. I notice his own name is on the ownership certificate."

I said defensively, "It's not an expensive car. Loads of them cost more."

She ignored this. "Did you enjoy your lunch?"

"No. It was awful. I ran out on them." Something half-hidden and yet still visible in her face made me suspect she knew everything and was sympathetic. "You've talked to them; haven't you?"

"Naturally, they called me when you ran out on them like that."

I hated to say it but the truth had to be brought out in the open. "Did they tell you what it was all about?"

"Morgan told me."

"I hate him!"

She put her hand out, as if to touch my shoulder, but our family wasn't very demonstrative and she drew it back and said instead, "You hate him now. But people like that aren't worth hating. It's his way of life. Something he was probably born with, like a cleft palate."

"No!" I yelled angrily. "I don't mean Jacques. I mean that Morgan Haight."

"Really? I'm told he's extremely eligible. A handsome fellow with excellent background. The Forresters consider him quite a catch."

"He's handsome. But he's awful. Anyway, Ann won't have as marvelous a time out of her marriage as I got out of mine."

She caught the past tense I used, and this time she did put her arm around me in the old, dear way of my childhood upon rare occasions, and it never failed to move me. I didn't want to cry but her gesture gave me that last push into a whole torrent of tears, while she patted me in a friendly, comradely manner, on the back.

"Don't worry now, Kay. It's all over. You've learned your lesson early. Every woman has a Jacques Levescu in her life, at least once. I did myself."

I looked up, sniffing and then wiping my eyes on the Kleenex she handed me in her practical way.

"You, Aunty! You were fooled by a man like Jacques?"

She grinned. "Why not? Do you think I'm immune to the usual feminine instincts? It was a long, long time ago, when I was making the Grand Tour with Father and Mother. But I still remember how handsome he was. Had a duelling scar here along his cheek. Or so he claimed. The truth is, he'd gotten it from a girl he'd seduced and left pregnant. She nearly carved his face up, I was told. He was much handsomer than your Jacques."

"Did I hear my name spoken?" asked Jacques as he appeared in the doorway. "Ah, here is my own precious child." He tried to enfold me in his arms, but I avoided him and started past him into the hall.

"I want to talk to you, Jacques."

"Darling, you promised not to use that cold tone. It makes my name sound so ugly."

"Need any help?" Aunty called after us, a little anxiously, I thought.

"I'll handle it," I said and Jacques looked at me oddly, but he followed me up the stairs. For some perverse reason, all his endearments, all the things that had won me and thrilled me, now made me writhe with self-contempt. That I could have fallen for such a corny, obvious line!

By the time we reached Great-Grandfather's suite, and he held the door open for me, I was shaking with nervousness. I was a little sick to my stomach, as well. But I kept remembering Aunty and the man with the "duelling scar," and Mother with her own gigolo problems. Obviously, as Aunt Grace said, I wasn't alone in my misery. Jacques closed the door, locked it, and started to take me into his arms. I let him do so. Then, as he kissed me, a deep, probing soul kiss, I gave no response. Just stood there stiffly, looking at him.

He smiled at me, a tender, warm smile that made me think of all the good things we'd had together, the marvelously romantic times I'd known since I met him. There was also the sense of having this terribly attractive man love and protect and care for me as a husband, a father, a lover. . . . And I almost broke down and gave in to the insistent demand of my senses.

"What is it, sweetheart? Why do you look at your loving master like that? Is something bothering you? If it is, you must be frank and tell me. And I will take care of it for my precious slave."

It was not his manner, which remained polished, but the words themselves that shook me out of the spell he cast so skillfully. What a lot of experience he must have had!

I said, "You kiss divinely, darling. And I don't think you are a bit over-priced. Not a bit."

59

His fingers, instead of releasing me, dug into my forearms. He looked a bit white around the gills, and I observed with complete detachment that his limpid brown eyes were actually mud-colored.

"That is a very cruel and lying thing to say," he managed finally. He had to moisten his lips before getting it out, however.

His discomfiture made me think of all the times he had his way by relying on moods and pouting and behavior far more childish than my own. I laughed a little, because it was that or cry over the dream that had just ended, not with a crash, but with a slow, grinding disillusionment, because, of course, what Ann and Morgan Haight told me was only what I had known since I overheard Aunty's talk with my husband over the six hundred thousand dollars he demanded. Instead of defending myself against his hurt accusation, I threw out what seemed a complete non-sequitur.

"Darling, I really am curious about one thing: Why the odd figure? Why is it always six hundred thousand?"

This rocked him. He even flinched and I was sure he tried but failed to control the color that crept up over his face. Surely a gigolo knows he is a gigolo? But maybe they consider themselves superior to other men who lease out their sexual prowess, because their stud fees are higher!

"Who has been telling you these lies, my little one?" When he couldn't tell whether that had done any good, he went on, more nervously, with a kind of desperation that twisted my heart because my contempt for him was all intermingled with pity. "Darling, there was a girl, it is true, up the river out of New Orleans. And we were— that is, the marriage was annulled for the most cruel and wicked reason, because of my Rumanian blood, I know this. And it is a blood of which I can tell you quite honestly, I am not ashamed. No. Lily-Mae Beamish was turned from me by her parents, hard, selfish Creoles, thinking themselves my superiors."

I began to laugh and couldn't stop for a minute. I knew it was hysteria but I simply couldn't help myself.

"Oh—Jacques! You can't imagine how funny. Just see —I didn't even know about Lily-Mae Beamish. I was talking about Morgan Haight's sister-in-law in Dallas. Isn't it funny?"

He stared at me. He had long since taken his hands off me and it seemed, to my overwrought imagination, that his features were twisted into such revulsion as I had ever believed I could inspire in anyone. The thought of how he must have felt this way always, during our most beautiful and most intimate moments, made my whole body ache with the shame and the fury that I couldn't control. Dear God, how he must have hated his method of earning half a million dollars! I was so shamed that my hysteria drifted into a rude, taunting laugh.

"You ought to see your face, Jacques. But don't worry. You'll be paid. I think you overcharge for your services though. You aren't really *that* good, even in bed!"

His eyes glistened with insane and very brief rage. He brought the flat of his hand around, making an arc in the air as he slapped me so hard across the mouth I thought my teeth would cut through my upper lip. It hurt a lot, but I was exceedingly grateful for it. It was the perfect ending to a ridiculous education in love that I had received early but which would mark me for life.

I thought when I went contemptuously over to the door and unlocked it, that I had seen the last of Jacques Levescu, at least in private. It was a notion which proved just as wrong and just as ridiculous as our marriage had been. Men like Jacques Levescu are always with us, the leeches that four thousand years of human society have not exterminated.

61

SIX/

Jacques got his six hundred thousand. Both Aunty and I wanted the whole divorce handled as quietly as possible, and Jacques, being Jacques, wanted to hold out. At first, he insisted I apply for the divorce in California, and the thought of my being tied to him for a whole year after the interlocutory decree was horrible. I knew I could forget him better—stop wanting and needing him—if I got a Reno divorce, and I did so, with Aunt Grace beside me.

Jacques was in Reno one day to facilitate matters for us. Once he got half his six hundred as a down payment, he was perfectly honorable about going through with the divorce. And during the twenty-four hours he remained in Nevada, we saw what he did with the money he won from idiotic women like me. For one thing, he was madly superstitious about the figure "six." Each time he had won a settlement from a wife who wanted to get rid of him, he named this figure, and then—he gambled. On six. Once the divorce preliminaries were over, Jacques went down to one of the roulette tables in the hotel and, so far as Aunty and I could figure out, he never left that

62

table until the next day, and rumor travelled through the hotel that "the foreign fellow dropped over fifty thousand." If this was the case, he would soon be broke again. However, that was his problem. It would never again be mine, or so I thought.

I'd never seen fifty thousand dollars in one lump, and I thought of all I'd been taught about the uses of such money in charitable, educational and, in general, "sensible" ways. Aunty used to tell me as an antidote to Mother's extraordinary lack of sense about money: "This power was only given to our family on loan. It is to be invested, shared with those unlucky enough not to have had a shrewd, unbeatable Bart Amberley in their ancestry."

It just killed me when I remembered what my relatives had done, for the good of mankind, with fifty thousand dollars, multiplied many times, of course. And here I was, giving it away, taking food from the mouths of hungry people somewhere, in order to ransom myself from an unpleasant mess.

The sight of Jacques Levescu leaning over the roulette table all night, his eyes glazed with the gambler's blind, single-minded concentration, should have taught me a great lesson. And as far as gambling was concerned, his behavior was a warning to me in the immediate future. It is true that, some years later, during a period of great unhappiness, I found the tables and wheels of Monte Carlo similarly fascinating, but I was to discover that gambling was a way of life to Jacques, and his only source of revenue was foolish women.

On the day I got my divorce, Ann Forrester cut classes at Berkeley and flew up to be with Aunt Grace and me. We all felt an enormous relief over my freedom, and both Aunty and Ann wondered what I would do with it. Since I had always been a good student in subjects which I enjoyed, I felt I could make up what I had missed

63

of my first semester at Cal, and in the end, I did just that. I returned with fair success to the collegiate life and friends I had almost lost with my romantic but image-shattering marriage.

I still didn't like Ann's fiancé, Morgan Haight, but it was none of my business what she did with her life, and when, on a brisk, windy May afternoon, Ann and I graduated from Cal, she announced the date of her wedding, Morgan suggested to her that I be her matron of honor. Ann was quietly clever about it, as she had always intended that I should be her Matron, but she bowed to Morgan's wishes in the most wifely way. I felt like a hypocrite, feeling as I always did that Morgan disliked and disapproved of me, and even more, that I returned the compliment with interest. But there was no way I could get out of it without telling Ann the truth, which was impossible.

As for me, I had sworn off serious entanglements, somewhat to Aunty's concern, as she explained the night we came home from Ann Forrester Haight's wedding and reception.

"It's that tag they hung on me ages ago, Aunty. That "Richest Girl" thing. No man could live that down. So when I have a relationship with a man, from here on in, I've got to remember that money is in that relationship somewhere. It's got to be."

We were in Aunt Grace's dressing room, adjoining her bed-sitting room, and Chiye Mitsushima helped Aunty take off her chinchilla coat. The young woman did not seem to be listening, but I was sure she took in everything. Aunt Grace shook her head.

"That's because you've never known a man with an equal background. Take Sophie-Frederick's son. He's had all the disillusionments you've encountered. And more. The son of a reigning head of state. That's a blow you haven't suffered."

64

I grinned and said with meaning, "Oh yes, I have."

She got the point and laughed. "Well, Katy, some day Sophie and I will bring you and Stefan together. And that will be the day when you are adult enough to take a serious place in life. How would you like to be in Sophie's position one day, ruler of a principality, a woman of stature in a man's world?"

"That'll be the day, all right." I removed my elbow-length white gloves and blew into them in the old-fashioned way she had taught me. "Can you see me helping to rule a country? Even a country we could fit nicely into Golden Gate Park?"

"Yes, I can," she said surprisingly. "Last summer Sophie and I talked of almost nothing else. And one day, mark my words, the Princess and I will get you two together."

I said with a certain amount of pique, "Not if The Prince persists in going off to hunt tigers in India whenever there's a chance we may meet." I still hadn't gotten over the previous vacation before my senior year, when, on our European trip, Aunt Grace coaxed me to visit her old friend, Princess Sophie-Frederick, the autocratic democrat who ruled over the principality of Feldenstein. This, as I reminded Aunty, was the second smallest independent state in Europe, and little more than a comic opera setting to its many visitors, but for my aunt it held two endearing attractions. One, of course, was the presence of the Princess, now a middle-aged woman, who had been her roommate in a Swiss girls' school before the first World War. The other, equally important, was the fact that Sophie-Frederick's handsome and distinguished playboy son, Prince Stefan Nicolaievich had, for some as yet unknown reason, never married. It wasn't difficult for me to see what the two old schoolgirl friends had in mind for us. And from the effect my projected arrival had on the Prince, the idea was even more repugnant to him than to me. At any rate, I still hadn't met him. Nor did I want to!

After graduation, I apprenticed myself as secretary, general handyman and flunky to the head of our Amberley Overseas Projects, in which progressive farming, crop rotation, and new implements were used to advantage in the underdeveloped countries. And thus it was that my mother's letter to me from Hawaii, sent care of Aunty, was five weeks late in reaching me as I returned from the interior to Nairobi.

Somewhat to our surprise, Mother described violent maternal symptoms and simply had to have a visit with me, as soon as possible. She had been living in Hawaii for the last year, in an elaborate skyscraper suite several blocks from the beach, but her lanai view took in the western half of Waikiki, from the nearby Ala Wai Canal to the surf itself. And as she had just divorced her latest husband, she was "starved for my naughty daughter's company."

It was March, the off-season for Hawaii, but even in the off-season, the whole island of Oahu was jammed with Malahini—the newcomers, visitors from the mainland. I was not anxious to return. After all, I told Aunty, I had been to Hawaii many times every year since I could remember, and each time, as it seemed to me, the Hawaii I loved became more strange, more hideous, more like Florida's Gold Coast. As I mentioned this to Aunt Grace, however, I realized that she didn't really want me to go and visit Mother. I wondered if it could be a kind of jealousy, that she was afraid I might grow fonder of Mother than of her. Aunty had raised my father and had never, I felt sure, quite approved of the marriage, though Mother's background was flawless from the standpoint of her social set. I always suspected that there was more to it than Mother's position in Café Society, the forerunner of today's Jet Set. Aunt Grace probably resented the appearance in the Amberley family of a woman as beautiful as Mother was.

In spite of the fact that Mother hadn't asked to see me in three years, I was frankly anxious to meet and get to know her again. My shameful episode with Jacques Levescu had revealed all sorts of weaknesses in me that, I thought, might be inherited from Mother. It was even possible that we might become close friends, confidantes. That would brighten my shrinking world of trusted friends, since Mother could scarcely have any ulterior motives in asking to see me.

Aunt Grace was running down poor Mother as usual, even at the Matson docks where she came to see me off.

"Myra's letter is filled with this new chauffeur of hers, Mike-Somebody. Try not to let it go too far, and don't go too far over those beachboys yourself."

"Well then, Aunty, I promise faithfully not to be seduced to the wild, extravagant night life and love of Myra Amberley. Now, take care of yourself while I'm gone."

It was awkward that Aunt Grace didn't laugh at my little joke. She took my meeting with Mother much more seriously than I did. "Your mother has asked me to recommend a young woman to supervise matters, the cleaning woman, the meals, the catering, Myra's own maids, and so forth. So you will have to leave Chiye there when you return. Chiye wants to go back to the Islands anyway, to visit her family. And this job will be a step up. Mostly supervisory."

"Who's going to pay her salary while she's with Mother?" I asked cynically.

She smiled. "Who do you think? At any rate, it won't do you any harm to dress and care for yourself on the return voyage."

67

She seemed to have forgotten my months in Tanzania and Zambia last fall and winter. I had been too busy to need the usual adjuncts of my more social friends.

"Have a good time, girl. And don't spend all your money in one place."

It was a standing joke among us, and it came from Aunt Grace's father who had landed in San Francisco, absolutely penniless, fresh off a bedraggled Cape Horner, and had started the Amberley fortune by selling the clothes off his back. Being a far-seeing man, he had come well equipped with them, the very latest, only six months old, from the fashion centers of New York. But he never forgot that poverty was a very real thing, not just something to be boasted about in one's past. And Aunt Grace had carried on the tradition.

It was only with the entrance of Mother into the family that money began to flow out . . . drift away into the maintenance of useless, unlived-in estates, a dark though expensive apartment on Sutton Place, a villa near Villefranche given over almost totally to the caretakers in between Mother's infrequent visits. There had been a Paris apartment, but Mother suffered some sort of dreary experience with her third husband there and had gotten rid of it.

"I promise," I said and kissed Aunt Grace on the cheek. "I wish you were coming along."

"Can't afford it," she said brusquely, and then added, with a bright light in her blue eyes, "Besides, if I were going, I'd fly."

It was so like her!

I always cry when sailing away on some romantic ship. All ships are romantic to me, and it didn't help that I could see Aunt Grace's small, indomitable figure closely wrapped against the incoming evening fog, in her six year old sables. It was too cold to stay on deck very long after we passed under the Golden Gate Bridge; so

I went across to my suite which smelled a bit like a funeral parlor, what with several vases of flowers, mostly roses, crowded into the bedroom and spilling over onto the lanai cocktail table.

Chiye was hanging my clothes, efficiently, but without enthusiasm, as she had performed every chore since I first knew her. She gave me an inferiority complex with her example of unshakeable calm. I had often tried to imitate this calm during my light relationship with men friends, dates, and would-be suitors. Gradually, something of the Oriental serenity I so envied seeped into my outward composure, but not quite as I had hoped. It crystalized the hardness, the disillusion I had acquired from the failure of my first marriage, so that the only people whose attentions I did not find suspect were the men and women of financial background similar to my own. And a dull crowd they were!

Except during my African experience, when I seemed to be in quite another, more vivid and purposeful world. There, only my newly acquired knowledge of farm equipment, and my ability to handle the bookkeeping plus shorthand and typing, were worth anything among strangers. That had been glorious, but—"let's face it," I had admitted to Ann upon my return, "I really like all the material things that go with being Kay Amberley."

"You can't be both," Ann reminded me in her common sense way. She always said things like that.

Chiye Mitsushima finished her work and stood staring at my back. I was at the dressing table brushing my hair after the lashing it had taken during my time on deck, and I saw her peculiar, expressionless eyes fixed on me. I longed to ask her why she disliked me, or if, indeed, she disliked *me* at all. She behaved this way to everyone.

"I won't need you any more tonight, Chiye. You must have your own unpacking to attend to. Is your cabin pleasant?"

69

"Very nice, M'em." She went to the cabin door, stopped "The roses in the blue vase are from a lady on board. The boy who delivered them said the lady and her husband are in Cabin 219. The name is Sebastian."

"Never heard of them," I said crisply, and Chiye left. More and more, I found myself using this cool, business-like tone which concealed something worse than indifference. It concealed suspicion. . . . Who the devil were the Sebastians? And why, since I didn't know them, had they gone out of their way to contact me, with gifts yet? The flowers were distinctly ornate. The stems long and perfect, the roses a flawless and deep, though waxy red. Blood red. Feeling ashamed of my own suspicions, I wondered what these Sebastians wanted from me.

The other flowers, including three corsages—all orchids and very much alike, had been placed by Chiye on my small ice chest. They were from friends like Ann and her new husband, various escorts I had known in college or the members of the local Cotillion Set which I had crossed up when I couldn't "come out." I was in Africa at the time, living what I called "real life," and somehow, the entire business of making a debut was pretty absurd anyway, when I had already been married and divorced.

An hour later, having changed to a black lace shell, higher heels and an unobtrusive set of diamonds, I went down to the Veranda Bar where one of the bar stewards on duty turned out to be Gus, who had known me for nearly twenty years. I had gone through the "milk for our little girl" period, the "Shirley Temple cocktail with lots of cherry juice" to the "coffee-Coke" period.

"You know, it's kind of sad to hear you all grown up and ordering Mai-Tais, Miss Amberley." Nobody ever called me Mrs. Levescu, thank God! But I understood Gus' nostalgia.

"Those were the days, Gus. I wish I could be that young and that naïve again."

"You shouldn't say that. You know, you've turned into a real beauty, these last few years." He set the big Mai-Tai down and I began to sip it through the straws. I gave him my best smile over the compliment, while I reflected wryly that he should have seen me a few months ago, riding a Land Rover in the African veldt, the natural champagne blonde of my hair a natural dust color, my face sunburned, my knees and elbows skinned raw, and my flesh a mass of welts from every conceivable insect bite. It had taken quite a few sessions at the Arden Salon in town to get me in shape for Gus' compliments. I did not say so, though. I had, at least, learned that much.

"Going over to visit your Mother, I suppose," he remarked, mechanically wiping off the little mosaic-topped cocktail table. "How is she making out with the Australian cowboy?"

"Good Heavens! That was months ago." I said airily, the only way one could handle Mother's marital excursions. I had long ago sworn that I would never-never in a million years, treat marriage the way Mother did. Unfortunately, with Jacques, I had made a good start toward Mother's goal.

"That's too bad," said Gus and he went off to take the order of a slightly seasick couple. We were out past the Farallone Islands by this time, crossing what would probably be the most choppy part of the Voyage. When Gus passed me again, he whispered in stentorian tones, "What happened? Don't tell me a guy walked out on Myra Amberley!"

I wasn't sure myself, but as we were attracting considerable attention from the dozen or so other passengers in the Bar, I explained what very likely was near the truth. "I believe he's been replaced by her new chauffeur." Although I had done scarcely more than whisper, I knew the woman facing me, at the next table, had looked up at mention of Mother's name.

She was noticeable in any case, with a thin, elegant, foreign-looking face framed in fine-spun, red-gold hair. Her expression was odd, dissatisfied, I thought, and querulous. But a minute later, as the ship heeled over a very little, the woman put a delicate handkerchief to her lips and closed her eyes. Embarrassed at my stupid mistake— she was obviously seasick—I raised my glass and tried to bury my thoughts in it. I was oddly depressed. How many sailings I had made in my girlhood, but always with people I loved! I was lonesome. That was the silly truth. And this seasick beauty, seasick or not, was sharing a table with a man. I could only see his back, but I envied her all the same.

Gus came back a couple of times to gossip with me about the old days, and finally showed up with a drink I hadn't ordered.

"Compliments of Mr. and Mrs. Sebastian," Gus explained.

I looked around, with the beginnings of real interest. Since I'd already been softened by one Mai-Tai, I began to think, selfishly enough, that I could use a few friends. Gus moved away from me, gesturing rather obviously over the head of the frail, elegant foreign beauty who had been staring at me, and over the man whose face I could not see. The frail beauty raised her frail eyebrows and ever so faintly waved her handkerchief. I had never thought of myself either as muscular or athletic, but before the fragility of this Dresden creature, I felt at an unusual disadvantage, for me.

The woman I took to be Mrs. Sebastian said something to her husband in answer to my smile and my panto-mimed toast to her as I motioned Gus to invite them to my table. The man hesitated, then turned around and in almost the same instant, stood up. He too was interestingly foreign, though neither young nor good looking, his thin face dominated by a prominent nose, very Italian, very authoritative. I wondered why we stared at each other, unblinking. I certainly had never seen him before; yet, there was this odd feeling that I knew him, and had known him. When? Where? There was no tie between us. I couldn't imagine why I stared. His smile as he and his wife came over to me was cool, a polite smile only. No more. Like the appraising look in his blue-gray eyes.

I shook off the curious sensation that had held me motionless a few seconds before, and greeted the two Sebastians with more enthusiasm than I could have imagined possible an hour earlier. At the same time, I was quite aware of my own hypocrisy, as this change of mood seemed to me. And I made up my mind now to be as congenial as possible to the Sebastians.

I thanked them both for the flowers, promised myself to send champagne to their table at dinner, and asked them if they were staying long in the Islands. I was still trying, discreetly, to find out their acquaintance with my family, when the woman mentioned Tijuana and then, with a sickening revival of an old pain, I remembered who they must be.

"*Pardon*," the woman said suddenly in French, having stopped in mid-sentence. She went on as before in English, "Have I said something? You look very strange."

I was about to admit the truth, that I had only just recognized them, when the man filled the awkward breach.

"I am afraid Miss Amberley remembers us as the betrayers of her elopement. What is called, I believe 'the stool pigeons.'"

I slapped my ice-chilled hand against my forehead and apologized.

"What an idiot I am! You must be Aunt Grace's
73

friends, the Grand Prix Winner, Luc Sebastiani. . . .
And you, Mrs. Sebastiani—"

"Claire," the fragile woman corrected me. And I recalled Aunt Grace's praise of her beauty which Aunty had not overrated. But Claire Sebastiani's eyes were golden, with disconcertingly feline irises. Sometimes they narrowed to slits, and yet the pale, almost transparent lips smiled consistently.

"I was told the name was Sebastian. It was stupid of me not to guess." I excused myself and laughed ruefully to let them know the old Tijuana-Levescu episode was a mere youthful peccadillo, and practically forgotten.

"I've seen only one Grand Prix. Two years ago. At Brands Hatch."

"Ah—yes." He nodded. "A good place to view the crucial—points. Unfortunately, I have never been able to take a First in England."

"It's a terrifying profession, Mr. Sebastiani. Are you going to race somewhere in the Islands?"

"Hardly." And this time he smiled, but the easing of his facial muscles, unlike the case with most people I knew, did not soften the web of fine lines around his eyes, or the reddened, leathery look of his face. He seemed always alert, tense. Never relaxing. There was not an ounce of extra flesh in his face, but the bone structure, while severe, was interesting. In answer to my question, he explained, "With the traffic what it is in Honolulu, I would not dare to drive my own car!"

His wife and I laughed. I felt my spirits pick up enormously as Claire Sebastiani, using champagne as a cure for seasickness, made a light Gallic joke about brave men on the battlefield who couldn't face Paris traffic, and then suggested that we three share a table in the Dining Salon.

"I thought you said half an hour ago that you would never eat again," Luc reminded her.

74

She shrugged. "Do not be *imbecile, mon cher*. When has a *française* not eaten a good meal, eh? Now, Kay— I may call you Kay? You agree, we dine together?"

"Do not rush things," her husband admonished her with an odd, almost suspicious look. "Undoubtedly, Miss Amberley is dining with the Captain. We are not."

As a matter of fact, arrangements were usually made to seat me at the Purser's table, our families being old friends, but the Sebastianis seemed different from the usual passengers one met at any of the officers' tables. I was pleased with Claire Sebastiani's invitation, although a trifle puzzled over Luc Sebastiani's lack of enthusiasm. Possibly, he still thought of me as the silly, thoughtless person who had once run away with Jacques Levescu. However, his coolness was more than cancelled by his witty, convivial wife. She was the kind of woman with whom another woman really enjoys a good gossip, as well as stimulating trivia about fashions, and, of course, men. Then, too, any friends of Aunt Grace's had one great recommendation to me at the start.

After several days in which the Sebastianis and I were constantly thrown together, I found that, unlike other sudden friends, the Frenchwoman and her Corsican husband remained both intriguing and interesting. Even I knew such a friendship was a dangerous one, which involved a husband, a wife and another woman, and I was careful never to find myself alone with Luc Sebastiani for more than a few minutes. Sometimes this proved difficult as Claire suffered from migraine, low blood pressure and a condition of general weakness which she blamed on her undernourished childhood in Nazi-occupied Paris.

When, for the second morning in succession, Claire broke her own date with me for morning coffee and Danish in the Veranda Café, deputizing Luc in her place, I began to think our threesome, and especially the Sebastianis, a trifle odd.

75

SEVEN/

PARTLY BECAUSE I did find him an attractive man in some indefinable way, I was extremely circumspect with Luc, and even more so when we were alone. But I still found him hard to fathom. At first I thought he disliked me; yet as I grew to know him better, his mystery grew. He was a reckless man. In my perhaps meagre experience I had never known a man whose "profession" was more hazardous. And it was not even a profession, but a very costly avocation. He was Number One, as I understood it, in a team riding for Cortot, a French motor company rapidly growing in international prestige, thanks to track victories by a few men like Luc Sebastiani.

Little as I knew about racing in the tradition of the worldwide Grand Prix, I had an idea that most of the men involved were very young, compared to Luc. But maybe it had become a necessity to him, even his livelihood. He never discussed his personal feelings about it, or which devil of danger drove him on to what I considered an almost inevitable end in flames or a broken neck, or both.

On the morning when Luc showed up again to explain, briefly, abruptly, that Claire was suffering from migraine, I stared up at him.

"Isn't this a little bit silly?" I asked, watching him fill his coffee cup at the urn, pick up two small cinnamon buns, and sit down across from me.

His expression was a bit sardonic over his coffee cup, whether at my question or the prospect of another tête-à-tête with me, but he managed to deny my implication politely.

"Not at all. I enjoy American pastry. Of course," he added, not quite smiling, "your coffee is impossible."

That made me laugh and we were off to a pleasant start. I explained that it was foolish of Claire to keep making these coffee dates, obviously just to oblige me, or keep me company.

"You see, I got in the habit of early rising because I had eight o'clock classes at my university for several years and it takes time to get across the Bay. Now I find it hard to break the habit." At the same time, out of nowhere, I suddenly had a picture of Jacques Levescu back in the unlamented days, telling me that no girl of my status got up early to do anything. The fact that I liked to do so had no weight whatever.

It was obvious, however, that Luc Sebastiani did not see things in quite the same light.

"A good habit it is. Don't change it, if you please." He looked into his coffee cup as though reading the coffee grounds and said abruptly, "You are altogether mistaken, you know."

This was so rude I raised my eyes and blinked at him, wondering what he was talking about. He swizzled the coffee around in his cup, spilled several drops and carefully sopped them up with his small cocktail napkin. Then he looked at me. He had disconcerting directness at such moments and I found myself shaken inwardly. I could not guess why.

"You are altogether mistaken when you think I am here solely as my wife's . . . deputy."

I could not prevent the warmth creeping into my face, more from pleasure than embarrassment. At the same time I had a very strong sense of trouble, even of danger, and I assumed the root of it was the possibility that we might have the making of a triangle, if I didn't get hold of myself.

"I know," I said and smiled the most impersonal smile I could manage. "You are here for the coffee, of course."

"Of course," he agreed, playing on the correct note at once.

I searched frantically for impersonal subjects and came groping back to the obvious tourist-to-tourist question:

"Will you be visiting all the Islands, or just Oahu? Claire talks of friends in Honolulu, but—"

He shrugged. The little spark of young humor and excitement that briefly lighted his tense, sombre face had died out and I felt depressed at what remained. Depressed and concerned at my own depression. After all, I scarcely knew these people. Their troubles were not mine. Or should not be.

"The trip is for Claire. There is very little here for me. That is to say, there *was* . . . very little," he repeated and drank the coffee, dregs and all.

His manner troubled me so much I committed the indiscretion of prying. Something I myself loathe, and I hated it even then, when I was younger, and hadn't so much reason for hating it.

"Claire is wonderfully gay, and everyone on shipboard adores her. But she looks so fragile. I think, perhaps, she tries too hard."

He considered this, nodded, and then said, "You look fragile, yet there is strength in you. Claire's problem—"

78

He broke off, went on in exactly the same low voice, with its faint accent suggesting both France and Italy, "I wonder if there is anyone in the universe who has not a problem. Shall I tell you my problem? I have an irrational fear of city traffic. Isn't it so?"

I felt this was the most polite slap in the face that I could have been given and it warned me, very correctly, not to meddle. I should have listened to my own feelings about meddlers. Although my feelings were hurt, I did not want him to guess, and I very much wanted him to think he was just another chance acquaintance, somebody who, when I left Hawaii, would move as easily out of my life as he and his wife had moved in.

"As far as complexes are concerned," I laughed, "I have a prize lot. Really, it's hard for me to sort them out sometimes."

He smiled, and I wondered why I felt that his smile was insincere, though he himself was deeply sincere. "I am sure that is not so."

To calm any fears he might have that there would be any further prying into what I began to suspect were two very curious lives, I started to get up.

"I have some letters to write; so if you will excuse me?"

"Of course." He was on his feet at the same time and now, just as I started past him, he said abruptly, "I think I must tell you something. My wife believes you are proud and things will change in the Islands when you discover we are paying a visit to my friend, and Claire's friend, Mike Stannert. But I think you should know."

"Who the devil is Mike Stannert?" I was more amused than surprised. Could this reticence of theirs explain the mystery about the pair?

"But I thought—Claire was sure you knew. He was on my Team three years. But there was much bad luck. And then a crash at Zandvoort and it was difficult afterward."

The morning breeze, whipping over the deck and

through the open door, was salty on my mouth and I moistened my lips. I saw that Luc had been gazing at my mouth and now looked away slowly with whatever thoughts he had well concealed behind an impassive façade. It made me nervous. I was more abrupt than I meant to be.

"I haven't the slightest idea who your friend is, and I honestly don't see how it concerns me, except that I'm sure he is a sterling character."

"He is presently employed by your mother, as her chauffeur."

The fullest implication of this disclosure didn't register at once. All I could think of was that the Sebastianis seemed to have a very low opinion of me if they believed I cut off friendships with people because they numbered chauffeurs among their acquaintance. Except for Aunt Grace, there wasn't a woman in the world I trusted as I trusted Hildy. And I didn't even know what servant's post she held, technically. For me, she held a position of respect similar to Aunt Grace's. Of course, I hadn't met this Mike Stannert yet. Maybe he wasn't worth knowing, but had an idea that Stannert must be a rather nice person if he was Luc Sebastiani's best friend. I said so aloud.

"He must be a nice person. I'll be glad to know him. . . . See you and Claire later. I'll be at the pool before the picnic lunch."

"Thank you, Kay. I told Claire it would not matter to you. About Stannert, I mean."

I said lightly, "What else?" But by this time I remembered something less pleasant about Mike Stannert. People spoke to me as I left, and I was glad of the chance to change the subject, but it didn't do much good. All the way to my cabin, I was thinking: "Good Lord! This Mike Stannert must be the chauffeur Mother is involved with. I wonder how much it will cost the Amberleys to get rid of him when she's changed her mind. And will Luc think less of me because we have to pay off his friend?"

Claire Sebastiani showed up at the pool sometime before noon, noticeably beautiful in her porcelain way, but since she gave an impression of such superiority over the rest of us women, I was not sorry to notice that her figure was meagre, to say the least, and that, like many Frenchwomen, she was heaviest in the wrong places. I remember feeling guilty over my own satisfaction at the sight, but, facially speaking, she would give anyone an inferiority complex. Her pale flesh looked positively transparent and her eyes—I think it must have been her golden feline eyes—made me feel uneasy whenever she glanced my way, which was often. I have always adored cats, but when I suddenly glimpse an animal's soul in what should be a human face, I can't help feeling the chill of the unknown, and the unnatural. Aunt Grace would laugh her head off at the idea. I rather suspected, though, that Mother wouldn't.

On the rare occasions when Mother invited me to visit her, I sensed the same quality that was so strongly a part of Claire Sebastiani's makeup. In Mother, of course, it was the merest touch of the "cat," quite human, and rather fascinating. I could almost always out-guess Mother, by reasoning as my dear old cat, Hepsibah, would have reasoned. But Claire Sebastiani puzzled me, and, in this strange way I have described, she made me uneasy.

On that particular, sunny March day, Claire came around the tile edge of the pool, cleverly and romantically swathed in a white lace robe over her bikini.

" 'Allo, Kay. You find the water pleasant?"

I said I did, and swam over to the side of the tiny pool where I held onto the tile and looked up at her. I was still laughing because I had been thoroughly splashed in the face by one of my fellow swimmers, a young bank teller from Anaheim, California.

"Come on in," I suggested gaily and then ducked and

81

yelled as my bank friend nearly drowned me with an enormous splash. He dived under the blue water and made a grab at my ankle. While I was cheerfully trying to fight him off in order to answer Claire's questions about what I intended to do in the Islands, her husband came out from the Veranda Bar. He strode along the tile, balancing two cocktail glasses, one of which he gave his wife who put out a frail hand and gracefully relieved him of the splashing burden. She drank rapidly, though not greedily. She never did anything in the crude way and would not, I was sure, carry on like a noisy child in the pool as I did. But for me in those days, and even later, fun was fun, wherever you found it, and as I was distinctly allergic to hangovers, I often enjoyed the childish antics like our pool battle more than the long, drinking parties of my harder-headed friends.

"A little pre-luncheon aperitif," Luc suggested, kneeling by the pool and handing me the second Champagne Cocktail. Then, as I balanced the glass, trying to sip and still fight off my bank friend in the pool, Luc brought over one of the deck chairs for his wife. He himself, though fully dressed in American slacks, a sweater and rope sandals, knelt between his wife's chair and the spot where the fingers of my right hand clutched the tile. He was close enough to get splashed from my friend and merely laughed, one of the few times I had seen him spontaneously amused. It might have been the superb weather for March, with the sky never more blue, but getting a large assist from the choppy waters through which we could see the clean white wake of the ship.

Claire, however, ducked back, frantically trying to avoid contamination from a few water drops. It was the realization of her obvious dislike for all this foolishness that made me decide I was too old for such going's on. Besides, I wanted to dry off, or sun-off, before getting into the line that was already forming in the Veranda

Bar for the buffet luncheon. I threw one last, enormous splash at my friend and then started to climb out, dripping wet, assisted by a shower of water from behind me in the pool. Luc gave me a hand up, and I was not blind to the expression in his always attractive eyes as he looked me up and down while I laughed and pointed out that I hadn't spilled a drop of my champagne.

Nevertheless, I was careful not to find myself on the tile between him and his wife, though Claire kept repeating, for some mysterious reason, *"Ici,* Luc, *mon cher.* It is dry here on the deck between us. You will get Kay a chair, please."

Luc hesitated, then moved away from his wife, leaving space for me, to my discomfort, while he brought over a second deck chair and I had to sit in it. I made up my mind I would leave as soon as I could, politely. The other reason I could give for Claire's curious way of throwing her husband at me, was an attempt to flaunt her own power over him, her complete confidence in his love. If so, and if she did this often, she played a dangerous game.

Luc, having settled me in the chair, knelt at my side and spoke of the beauty of the weather, and so gave me a chance shortly to shake myself off, claim I had to get out of my wet suit, and leave them. When I did go, and looked back to wave casually in their direction, I was conscious of her bright, feline eyes—thinking what? What do cats think when their glowing, unblinking gaze engulfs you? And I was conscious, as well, of Luc Sebastiani looking at me, his gaze very different from that of his wife, thoughtful and warm. I tried not to be aware of it.

Chiye Mitsushima was in my suite packing for the following day's arrival in Honolulu, and I sent her up to join the group at the Veranda Buffet for lunch. She smiled for the first time I could remember, although, so far as I knew, she had gone to every buffet she cared to. I didn't really need her on the trip, and had never made much call upon her time on board. I myself delayed going back to the Veranda, spending a long time in the shower towelling dry, putting on a last year's orange and gold Hawaiian sun-dress, strapless in the fashion of that time, and elasticized around the breast of the dress. When I returned to the buffet everyone was half through eating, and I was fortunate enough to meet my bank teller friend who loaded a tray of creamy potato salad, shrimp salad, delicious, tart, lomi-lomi salmon, slices of ham and turkey, slices of tomato, barbecue beans, a wedge of cocoanut cake and a tall glass of iced tea. All this he claimed he had acquired for me and looked around for two seats at one of the cocktail tables.

"Hey! There we are!" he cried and led me on a twisted path between the tables, precariously balancing my tray above bobbing heads. Too late, I saw who had raised a hand, signalling us to join that table. It was Claire Sebastiani, of course, and with her Luc, astonishingly enough, was Chiye Mitsushima. It was not some snobbish notion of her inferior position that made me surprised to see her there, but the fact of her acquaintance with them which, until now, had been a secret from me. Her impassive face was lighted, beautiful, her eyes absolutely sparkling. With vivid gestures she was describing something to Luc who listened to her but seemed to have half his attention on us as we made our way toward their table.

I tapped my friend, Bob, on the back.

"Isn't there another table? That one seems to be pretty busy."

He looked around, confused, and by the greatest bit of luck, a man and woman in half-dried swim suits got up in front of us, leaving their trays of empty dishes, and Bob and I almost fell into the chairs. I waved to the Sebastianis at the next table beyond us and said, "Marvelous food; isn't it?"

84

Claire replied, pleasantly as ever. Luc and I exchanged long, expressionless glances which I, for one, felt carried in them a complete understanding. He knew why I was avoiding him, and he knew too, that our avoidance of each other indicated a mutual feeling we did not want to build on. Eventually, as our awkward little picnic progressed, the conversation at the table behind us picked up where our appearance had given it a prolonged interruption.

"You were saying, Chiye?" Claire's silvery voice cut into the light chatter in the room. "You say the boy is fine and bright and healthy?"

Astonished, I listened without appearing to. It seemed incredible that Chiye Mitsushima, whom I had known for seven years, was talking about a child. Whose child? And how long had the Sebastianis known her? They had not once mentioned her to me.

"It is hard, Madame Claire. But it was harder before. When my mother was sick, that was hard. It was so long before she was better. And so expensive! Now, she is well again and takes good care of the boy."

I was shocked to think that impassive, inhuman Chiye Mitsushima had a son! And those financial problems. That was shameful. Did we pay such low salaries that a woman couldn't support a child and a sick mother? It began to occur to me, belatedly, that it would be my fault if such things happened in future. Aunt Grace ran my life, my fortune, my household, and ran them well, but she ran them in the way that was to be expected, like a woman born at the end of the Nineteenth Century. I was born to the era in which we lived. I was going to have to take over my responsibilities.

Obviously, something would have to be done about Chiye Mitsushima's salary, if her family was being allowed to starve, or very near that. So many things to investigate, to check, to learn all about. . . . How skilled

85

Aunt Grace had been, to take on all this and at an early age! Meanwhile, I still found puzzling the curious relationship between the Sebastianis and Chiye.

But very soon Chiye's problems ceased to interest me. The final night out, after a good deal of festivity, champagne and Black Russians at midnight, Claire asked Luc to leave her at their cabin and escort me to mine.

"It is not necessary," I assured Claire. She seemed to be embarrassingly interested in my spending no time alone. "I think I'll enjoy some of that balmy midnight air on deck. I'm still a romanticist at heart."

I couldn't help being aware of the unspoken quarrel between her and Luc, his refusal to obey some signal of hers. I tossed them a gay good night and went up the grand staircase to the promenada, and then an outside companionway to the Boat Deck.

How calm the dark, deep Pacific looked at midnight when the ship's lights were dimmed and nothing but the stars illuminated the long path that lay between our little ship and the enormous stretch of the South Pacific! I caught myself wishing I could share this incomparable night with someone . . . very special. It was quite a shock when the very voice, the face and presence that peopled my thoughts, suddenly interrupted my reverie.

"Is there anything more beautiful than such a night in such a place?"

Luc Sebastiani's shadow fell across my face as I turned. He was smiling. His eyes seemed to burn into my very soul. As I caught the contagion of that rare smile, he added, "And in such company?"

"Now, you do sound French," I murmured.

We stood there staring out at the sea and deeply aware of the hot surge of our blood, as our hands met, and then our shoulders, mine bare and chilly only moments before, now warmed by his presence.

"You know she wants this?" he said presently.

86

"But why?"

"It is a long story. And ugly. Never mind. She expects us to go below. To your cabin."

I looked up at him. The moonlight was full in my face and he must have seen my eyes shine with my desire for him. Breathless, and with my lips moistened in my nervousness, my craving, I murmured, "It need not be below, in my cabin. Wouldn't it be a marvelous joke on her if . . . up here . . . on deck. . . ."

He took hold of my shoulders so hard I winced, as his eyes fixed their deep gaze on something behind me, against the ship's funnel.

"Here?" he whispered.

There was no need for me to answer. I don't remember moving to the forgotten blue deck chair behind us. I only remember we were there. The dark, hard shadow of Luc's body hiding me from the world. It was all a mad, sweet haze of feelings, sensations, the bright, luminous, unforgettable pain of my longing satisfied. The brief, so brief yet perfect seconds during which he prepared my tense flesh to welcome his love.

Sensations crystalized, burning within me, a fire in which I felt he was consumed.

We were suddenly still. And we knew a rare, emotional response had been shared. The nearness of danger, of discovery roused us, even as it had earlier given us the final fillip of sensation.

When, a bit shaken by our experience, we descended later to my deck, we separated there, not even looking at each other, but our fingertips touched, briefly, and then I hurried along to my cabin. I appeared to be pleasantly surprised and was, in fact, amused when, shortly after I entered my cabin, the door opened abruptly behind me and Claire Sebastiani stood there in a very sheer negligee, looking distraught, her thin, pale flesh shadowy and probably tantalizing beneath the sheer garment's folds. I could imagine her surprise, and I still didn't know why she wanted to frame me with her husband.

"Hello, there," I called out, dumb and innocent. "Thought you'd gone to béd."

"I—I wondered if you would join me for a drink. I have—the insomnia."

I smiled and stretched my arms over my head luxuriantly.

"Not I. I feel as though I could fall asleep the minute I hit the bed. *Bon soir . . . chérie.*"

"Yes . . . I see."

She didn't, of course, but she left.

And I went to bed. But I had lied, too. I wasn't in the least sleepy. I spent hours trying to re-live and re-experience those moments in the deck chair when I had Luc's precious symbol of his virility in my care, in my warmth, and he was mine, so briefly.

EIGHT/

LOVING AS I DID the Honolulu greeting to its Matson Line passenger ships, whose vivid memories went back to my earliest childhood, I never travelled on the freighters of our own Amberley subsidiaries in the Pacific. Often, I had made this trip with Aunt Grace, even as recently as two years ago, because she was such a good companion, meaning she left me alone at times to live that young, gay, romantic life I had almost forfeited by my early marriage to Jacques Levescu.

I was surprised to see Mother down on the dock, in the crowd, waving to me, near where the beloved Royal Hawaiian Band was playing. I hadn't deliberately avoided the Sebastianis, but I did not see them until we were disembarking some minutes later, all of us pleasantly drowned in cool, damp, exquisite-smelling flower leis. Chiye was with me, carrying my old, scuffed jewel case, while I carried a stole, an item I usually brought against the advice of my Kamaiiana friends, the Islanders, who insisted it never rained "rain" and it never got chilly. I knew perfectly well that Mother wouldn't be caught

89

dead with me if I didn't have at least a mink or sable stole with me. I was still a little intimidated by Chiye. I wanted to ask about her family and yet, even when given the opportunity last night, as she helped me to dress for the formal Captain's Ball, I had put off questioning her. She never looked receptive to me. Besides, after my unforgettable moments with Luc, I was afraid Chiye might guess what had happened between us.

Coming down the gangplank and then down the steep dark way into the sheds, for this was before the very modern building and escalators of today, I looked around into the crowd below me, pleased and flattered when I again found Mother's beautiful face looking up at me. I still didn't know why she was there. She seldom put herself out, even for me, and several times that morning while I was telling myself it was good of her to come down to the docks and deck me with one more, and especially lovely pikaki lei, I remember having not one really filial feeling about her. After more than twenty years of intermittent experience with her, I found so little emotion we had in common that it sometimes seemed impossible we could share the same blood.

If that was the case, Mother intended to alter old custom, old ideas in one large and uncharacteristic leap. She pushed her way through the crowd to me, and really put everything into the hug and kiss she gave me. I was less surprised at this when several flash bulbs exploded and I didn't need to look around to guess "someone" had informed them that there was a special significance to our meeting. Suspicion deepened in me at once.

What did she want? Not my company, certainly.

Mother had lightened her deep auburn hair and the heavy tendrils that had been shoulder length for rather too many years were now entrancingly short, curly and youthful. Her mouth always seemed extraordinarily

90

sensual, large and full, carefully moist, but she was wearing a very light and silvered lipstick which brought out innumerable creases in her lips. I wished I knew her well enough to tell her so. She was wearing a belted, full length white mink coat which seemed a bit much, even to a Mainlander like me.

"Hello, doll. How was the voyage? Seasick at all?"

"Of course not, Mother! I love it. You're looking fine. I like your hair."

"Call me Myra, dear." She draped another lei around my neck just as a flashbulb went off. "Myra sounds better, now that you are so grown up and all. I simply can't imagine anyone taking the stodgy old boat when you can fly. Come along. Mike is picking up your luggage."

"You sound like Aunt Grace," I said and then blinked as another picture was snapped. I had been caught in a mouthy shot as we walked chummily out of the sheds. "She wants to fly everywhere and then complains about being stuck for hours in strange airports or stacked above strange cities."

Mother wrinkled her elegant nose. "That's because she's so old, dear. She's afraid to take a boat. She might die before she gets there."

"Meow," I said.

We had reached the car. "Not a Rolls! Oh, Mother! Good Lord!" She reminded me suddenly of Jacques Levescu. What a pair they would have made!

"Myra . . . dear. Myra! Here's Mike now."

I looked around, expecting the worst, a kind of Irish-faced gigolo. Instead, I saw a very tall, pleasant young man, well put together—no mistake about that!—who was loading my bags in, as he gave me a big, infectious grin. Then, as Mother introduced us, I noticed Luc and Claire Sebastiani passing behind the ostentatious black car, and I waved to them. They had apparently not in-

91

tended to intrude on my meeting with Mother, even to speak with their friend, Mike Stannert.

"I met some friends of yours on shipboard, Mr. Stannert," I said. "Mother. . . . Myra—" I hastily amended, "Here are two of my distinguished fellow passengers, the Cortot Team's Grand Prix Winner, Luc Sebastiani, and his lovely wife." Almost before I could get out Mother's own name—she returned to the "Amberley" name after each divorce—she almost fell on Luc's neck.

"Of course, I have heard of Luc Sebastiani! My dear man, I was at Monte the day you made a First. That was when your teammate had that appalling accident. Kay, he simply dissolved in flames!"

Everybody changed the subject, with a welcome assist from Chiye Mitsushima who luckily, in my opinion, dropped my jewel case. No harm was done. The container was a beat-up old makeup case that had a clever and almost foolproof lock, which made the whole thing look scarcely worth stealing. I had worn Grandmother's emerald parure at the Captain's Ball but thought it unlikely I would wear it in Honolulu. Things were not that formal here. But the ensuing scuffle for the case, between Mike Stannert, Chiye and Luc, gave us a welcome change from the subject of men who "went up in flames."

Mother invited the Sebastianis up to her apartment for cocktails that afternoon and Clare was just on the point of agreeing when, to everyone's surprise, Luc said they had a prior engagement. It was an awkward moment, and was both glad he refused the invitation and sorry at the same time. His single glance at me told me why he was refusing. I tried to let him know, by the expressionless return of his glance, that I understood. It was embarrassing to be caught at this by Mike Stannert's lively eyes. He looked from me to Luc, then frowned a trifle, and finished packing my bags in the car.

As Mother and I got in, and Chiye sat facing us in her quiet, impassive way, Mike stopped only a minute or two, exchanging some racing news with the Sebastianis. I heard him make a date with them for breakfast. I wished very much that, in other circumstances, I might be with them. Strange, though, the way Claire Sebastiani seemed to do everything possible to push us together!

I couldn't tell how Chiye Mitsushima reacted to Mother as a future employer. She was her usual calm self, although I saw her smile faintly as we all said goodbye to the Sebastianis who had, I was happy to see, attracted the photographers themselves. But I was too busy with my own reactions on the way out to the Waikiki district to pay much attention to Chiye.

The changes in Honolulu, particularly on the Waikiki skyline, were nearly as rapid and as alarming to lovers of the earlier Hawaii then, as they are today. I complained to Mother but I might have known what answer to expect. Every new high-rise meant a potential home for her, each more elaborate than the one before. She was so innocent, so transparent about it, I had to laugh and accept the fact that Mother was growing younger, less responsible every year, while I was going in the opposite direction. I felt years older than Myra Amberley.

"With Miss what's-her-name living in, dear, and handling my small staff, and then, of course, if I should happen to marry again—anything is possible, you know—well, I'll need a much larger apartment setup. And there really are some lovely little penthouses. . . . Nothing gaudy. You'll adore them!"

I could imagine! Mother went through over two hundred and fifty thousand dollars a year with no effort whatever, plus her investments, and still we paid off, just as regularly, the sizable loans she incurred.

I tried to make my remark lightly, but there was an edge to my voice and even Mike Stannert heard. I saw

93

him glance at me in the mirror and he didn't look away in embarrassment as other men might have, when he caught my eye. There was a clean, open frankness about his Irish face. He was not, I thought, the kind to play my mother for her money alone. Or if he did, he would tell her so.

During this revealing moment, I said to Mother, "I can imagine your 'little penthouse.' The way you live, and with your little retinue, you really need twin penthouses, side by side."

"Don't be sarcastic, Kay. You always were a disgusting little prig, even when—" Mother bit her lip and flashed her big smile. With a detachment I was sorry for, I noted once again how the silvery lipstick was so unflattering to her mouth when she smiled, or even when she didn't. She went right ahead being very young, the Irresponsible Debutante she must have been when father met her. It might be pitiful, except that she *was* my mother and of all the emotions, I felt she would hate most to be the object of pity from a younger woman.

She amended her "disgusting little prig" picture of me now so quickly I had to smile, and caught Mike Stannert's grin in the mirror. "That is to say, dear, it was stupid of me to criticize you. After all, what else could you be, in a house ruled by that—that old bitch?" Before I could make a wholly unnecessary defense of Aunt Grace, she rattled on, "In spite of Grace Amberley, you are looking marvelous, I must admit. A little thin, perhaps, but you'll grow out of it. Marriage will change all that."

We had pulled into the garage of a skyscraper apartment house a block off Kalakaua Avenue in the heart of the Waikiki district, but I was so startled that I almost didn't get out of the car until Chiye's cool voice urged,

"Excuse me, please. The man is waiting."

I was annoyed at the slight pressure she applied to the

94

small of my back, but "the man" Mike Stannert, had already helped Mother out and had a hand extended to me. I touched his hand very briefly and joined Mother. Brief as my touch was, I could hardly overlook the masculinity of his hand, the strength of it, and I thought quickly of ways in which such hands had been important, in those terrifying deadly races where Luc Sebastiani took equal chances with his life.

"What did you mean about my marriage?" I asked Mother. "I've had that. While I'm far from losing interest in men, I'm not about to buy myself another husband."

"I was talking about that good looking Prince of Feldenstein, of course. I met him last winter. But you musn't be crude, Kay. Talking about buying husbands and that sort of cheap thing."

"Not so cheap," I put in.

But I had certainly struck a nerve with Mother. My casual, if heartfelt, remark about buying a husband made her give me a very nasty look. I was glad the chauffeur was busy discussing the baggage problems with Chiye Mitsushima, because I was beginning to suspect that Aunt Grace's suspicions about Mother and Stannert were correct as usual. It was Mike who puzzled me. I might be prejudiced in his favor because he had once been on Luc's team, but somehow, I couldn't believe the Irishman was planning some devious gigolo effort. Whatever the man had in mind, it wouldn't be devious.

A few hours later, I wasn't so sure. I had seen and duly admired Mother's apartment which covered half the very sizable tenth floor, with its great view of the west half of Waikiki, its two lanais and enormous picture windows, the huge living room opening onto the lamais. . . . It was uncomfortably oriental. Mother had managed to substitute low tables, cushions, pads, even a cumbersome console television set, for every decently com-

fortable chair and couch. There was a great deal of
ebony, and I wasn't surprised to find her own bathroom
and bedroom black and white to a depressing degree.

It looked for a while as though Mother had forgotten
all about Chiye, and her other three servants were equally
indifferent. I had to remind her when Mike Stannert
came into the apartment foyer after the merest pretense
of a knock, and asked me with the first embarrassment I
had seen him exhibit, "I think the Japanese lady is waiting to be assigned her—quarters. Shall I ask M—your
mother?"

I was sure he had been about to call her "Myra," but
Mother's love life was, or ought to be, her own affair. As
a matter of fact, Chiye's quarters should have been her
affair too, but I felt the full responsibility of it. I had
brought the woman over, and I was beginning to suspect
I would be responsible in every way.

"I'll settle it with Mother. Please make her comfortable
until we can decide."

Mother left it entirely up to me, "As long as she is
close at hand. Mike, will you help my little girl straighten
things out with that tiresome manager downstairs?"

Mike took me down to see the manager who was just
directing a newsman and a photographer to the eleva-
tors, but seeing us, he called, "Hey! Here's Miss Amberley
now," and when I started to protest, he added, "You're a
kind of special visitor, Miss Amberley. They'll naturally
want your slant on the wedding and all."

The good looking young Japanese newspaperman
swung around, pinched his pal and hurried toward me. I
was dying to ask, "What wedding." But I could picture the
resulting havoc in the newspapers, so I tried to dismiss
their questions with the old reliable "no comment." While
they were still babbling about a wedding—Mother's name
kept popping up, of course!—I explained our problem to

the manager who was extremely obliging, and Chiye ended up with a small but very pleasant apartment on the eighth floor. Then I remembered.

"Is there room for her Mother and her child?"

There was a second bedroom. Everything seemed simple enough, and I was surprised at Mike Stannert's odd expression when I had signed for the apartment, issued a check and then asked with more calm than I felt, "Are we all through?"

"But about the wedding, Miss Amberley?"

"Later," I said. They snapped a couple of shots of me anyway, and it wasn't until Mike pushed me into the elevator, pressed buttons and put doors between ourselves and the press, that I felt free enough to demand to know, "What the devil is this wedding business all about? Or wouldn't you know?"

He gave me that wide-open grin I had noticed at the first moment of our meeting, and I was disarmed, though I kept my cynical expression.

"I ought to know, Miss A. I'm supposed to be the groom."

Flabbergasted at his frankness, I leaned against the rank of elevator buttons and we stopped our ascent with a sickening lurch.

"I could have guessed that! Let me ask you a perfectly straightforward question."

"I'll go for that." He reached over my shoulder, pressed the button for the tenth floor again and looked into my face. "If you want to throw a spanner in the works, you probably can."

He was one of those gay, easy creatures with whom it is utterly impossible to be angry. You might as well scream at an amoral infant.

"I suppose you are madly in love with Mother." I realized after I said this that I was not being very fair to Mother. But before I could amend this, Mike Stannert said, "Don't be nasty. I'm not madly in love with anyone. Never have been. But I do like the old . . . girl. And I'd as soon marry her as not."

His frankness made things both harder and easier. I decided to use his own tactics.

"I imagine you wouldn't be insulted by a bribe. If it were big enough."

"That's where you're wrong, Miss A. It's got to be money I earn, number one. And it's got to be something I can live with—or we can live with, and I can't live with a fortune. If I was looking for big money, there'll be a lot bigger bargains going right here in Honolulu, than Myra." I opened my mouth, but he beat me to the punch, his voice and manner pleasant, though I thought there was a good deal more seriousness in his expressive eyes than there had been a few minutes before. "You are thinking I'm some conceited goniff; aren't you? But believe me, people get lonesome. And rich women—sorry, Miss A!—get more lonesome, because they're used to folks around them. It just so happens I've gotten to like Myra. She's fun. She's kind of dumb and irresponsible maybe, but I do need the money, and I never was one to go for the brainy females. Or the bossy ones."

"Is that intended as a slap in the face at me?" I asked lightly as we stepped out into the foyer of Mother's apartment suite.

He took my arm very formally, mimicking the white-tie escort, and left me speechless with his contradiction, "You know, you are much sexier, and much less brainy than you think you are."

I knew I had been insulted, but I would have been much less a woman if I hadn't enjoyed it.

Mother was in the bar, mixing Martinis with the help

of an attractive Filipino boy who gave Mike Stannert a quick, hooded look that I caught. Mike looked at Mother, whose red hair was tousled but more attractive than ever. I was interested in the relationship between them, or at any rate, the sincerity of the relationship, and was glad to see that some sort of very real sympathy seemed to exist between Mike and Mother.

"Here. I'll do it." He took everything out of Mother's hands and finished the business himself. His masterful quality suited Mother. She liked to be overpowered and outmaneuvered—by a male. As a matter of fact, this sort of weakness I inherited.

"Guess what, Dear?" Mother asked me proudly.

She took her first long, pleasant sip of the frosted martini which was the product of her hand and that of her future husband, Mike Stannert. "Those marvelous Sebastianis have changed their minds. They'll go to dinner with us. She's a glorious-looking creature, isn't she? Claire Sebastiani, I mean."

"Was it Claire who called to say they'd changed their minds about the date tonight?" I wondered.

"Yes. How did you know? She said Luc changed his mind. I'm glad. Though frankly—" She looked at me. "It's his record, more than the man himself that intrigues me. One wonders why she married him. Unless he was famous then, of course."

I took the Scotch-on-the-rocks that Mike prepared for me, and noticed without looking at him, how interested he was in Mother's remarks. I remembered suddenly that he was an old friend of Luc's. Prodded by his interest, I said to Mother, "You don't think he's attractive?"

She was surprised. "Well, hardly! He hadn't a word to say for himself when we met. And from Claire's attitude, I assume it was Luc who didn't want to see us again."

"Curious," I said. "To me, he's one of the most attractive men I've ever met." I shrugged, very much aware of Mike's astonished stare. "But I suppose it's a case of—To each his own."

I did wonder why Mike seemed troubled over my remark.

NINE/

IT WAS an odd sort of evening. Several times, Mike seemed
on the verge of telling me something, "warning me," I
thought, very curious about it. But I couldn't figure out
all the endless little threads that seemed to be woven
among us all, Mike's anxiety to keep me away from Luc,
Claire's strange obsession to get us together, Luc's own
obvious attraction to me. I couldn't be mistaken about
that. There was something between us that each of us
knew, when we shook hands in their European style,
when we happened to glance at each other at the most
casual moments. . . . A dozen things that made each of
us aware of the invisible tie, the attraction to the other.
And just as surely, there was something that we wanted
to hide, even to destroy. I was not born, I told myself, to
aid and abet adultery. Of course, I was still quite young
in those days!

We went out to Diamond Head that night to a luau at
the Monarch Club, and everything was as it had been
long ago. There was the succulent baked pig and the pi-
quant lomi-lomi salmon, the endless side dishes and the

laughter and applause of the groups sitting cross-legged at the long, low tables, while I sat between Mike Stannert and Luc Sebastiani, wondering if this too was going to be one of Mother's endless marriage quests for something or other. I thought it conceivable she might be happy with Mike. His frankness, at least, was refreshing, and I was sure he genuinely liked her, which is more than one can say for some marriages I had observed. 'Happiness' would be the obvious answer, but some people have a genius for pursuing every experience that will lead to further failure, and in the end, unhappiness.

Selfishly, I was wondering if such patterns were inherited. I had miserably failed in my own marriage; yet I was now sitting between two men who attracted me in many ways, though I knew, even in those moments, that the attraction was very different. I liked Mike, in spite of everything I knew about him. And I could see that Claire, on Mike's other side, felt something similar about him. At least, she seemed to pay him a great deal of attention. I wondered if Mother noticed; I hoped she didn't. It would only complicate things for her.

As for Luc, almost from the first I had been drawn to him, and in his case, there was no need for charm or laughter or any of the other Irish qualities of the redoubtable Mike Stannert.

Mike talked to me often, making conversation to tease and enliven me when I began to be silent and wonder what Luc was thinking. And if I was in his thoughts at all.

"With all your money, Miss A, you couldn't buy this kind of a feed, that tasted this good, except on its home grounds."

"It has been my observation," Luc said, "that the more rich the Americans are, the more it is impossible for them to eat such food. The ulcers will not permit it."

102

I laughed. "In America it's ulcers. In France, it's the liver that gives the trouble."

"*Touché!*" cried Claire in her bright, tinkling voice. "And is it not so? How often have we not taken my *belle-mere*, Luc's mother, to the spa for her liver! She drinks too much, of course. That is understood."

"Drinks too much?" my mother echoed, leaping onto this scandalous disclosure with interest.

Claire was bland. "But yes. Too much of the waters at the Spa."

Mother raised her eyebrows, evidently feeling that she had been tricked in some way, and began to discuss matters of the household with Mike, which pointedly excluded the Sebastiani's and me as well.

Claire said to me, "we have another so dear friend in common, I think. The Princess Sophie-Frederick of Feldenstein. She was kind enough to send for Luc personally after Le Mans last year. We were given an audience. A most gracious lady. And her son, the Prince!" She rolled her glittering golden eyes. "Such a handsome man! One wishes at such times that one were free. I have known him since I was a girl."

Without intending to, I glanced at Luc who smiled back at me. He seemed genuinely amused but didn't explain why he found so amusing his wife's admiration for the man who would one day rule a principality.

"How does Prince Stefan Nicolaievich appeal to you?" he asked me, somewhat to my surprise.

"I can't say. I've never met him." Claire turned and stared at me quite frankly, so I went on. "With great effort and an enormous expenditure of time and money, His Highness and I have managed to just-miss each other on at least five, maybe six occasions."

He said goodhumoredly, "I find that hard to believe."

Claire burst into flutters of enthusiasm. "He speaks of

103

you with such enthusiasm, we expected at our next meeting we must curtsey to you. The Princess spoke of what I believe she called 'an arrangement' made many years ago between herself and your dear Aunt Grace."

"Good God!" Mother exclaimed, interrupting a close tête-à-tête with Mike. "So she's 'dear Aunt Grace' to you! I could tell you a choice item or two about Dear Aunt Grace. Couldn't I, Kay?"

"I wouldn't know," I said stiffly, and Luc was quick to take the hint in my voice. He began to question me about Europe, about my favorite spots, what I thought of the French . . .

"You sound like us Americans. I didn't know the French cared what we thought of them." He started to deny this, or I thought he was going to, and I added, still teasing him, "What can I say without insulting my grandmother? She was French. Many San Franciscans are."

"You are a chauvinist," he accused me.

"Like all the French."

Looking at each other, we both laughed and went on gazing at each other, and suddenly there was no laughter between us. It was beyond that. It was a curious moment, one I was destined never to forget. As if we had communicated our feelings without needing words and sounds.

It was Mike Stannert who came to our rescue, complaining that he hadn't had a drink in two hours and it was "time we all got oiled."

"That's my Mike!" Claire said surprisingly.

Mother gave her a look. But very soon we were all getting up off the ground, or close to it, amid grunts and groans, to debate where the best bars were. When Mother suggested a place far out beyond residential Kahala, I figured it was because she and Mike had often been there, but that only shows how little I still knew Mother.

This mysterious little bar managed to disappear while we were stumbling around in the cool spring darkness, and Claire was asking Mike for a botanical discussion of the magnificent night-blooming Cereus growing along the hedge and wall of a cliffside estate.

"Exquisite place, wouldn't you say, dear?" Mother asked me, with suspicious anxiety. The men were discussing the names of neighboring bars if any, with the caretaker of the estate behind the night-blooming Cereus wall. The ornate gates of the estate were open, and the caretaker had been found standing in the doorway of his cottage, calmly smoking a pipe, as if expecting visitors.

"How d'you like that?" Mike yelled at us. "The place is for sale. Two hundred thousand flat. No more. No less. What a view they must get from those lanais! And the bedrooms halfway down the cliff. . . . How'd you like to spend a honeymoon there, Myra, my girl?"

That was all Mother needed to claim she and Mike. . . . "And you too, Kay dear, must come back and look over the estate tomorrow."

Claire Sebastiani leaped in to support Mother's obvious campaign. The two women chattered about the place and what a bargain it was, an idea I shared, though with different motives; for the location, the long, winding drive downward to the shore, the lush spring foliage, and of course, everything Mother and Mike had mentioned about the main residence itself intrigued me. I was telling myself, "I might be happy here. I might build a little fortress against the world right here. And it would be impossible for intruders, photographers, nosey newsmen, to get to me without a good deal of trespassing."

Luc had been watching me. He said suddenly, "We were intended to come here tonight. You know that; do you not? I have no doubt the enthusiasm—and the rest —is for you to hear."

"And me to buy?"

He was puzzled. "You are not angry to be used? You don't resent it?"

"Why should I?" I very much wanted Luc Sebastiani, of all men, to think the best of me, but I wanted to be honest with him, of all men, as well. "I really think if I like it by daylight, I will buy it. But for myself. I never did a big thing like this alone in my life. But it's about time I began! I feel a new image coming on." I was flexing my fingers in my nervousness at my own daring, and he took my hands and held them warmly between his.

"Bravo! Begin to live your life. And don't let anyone cheat you again, no matter how much you love him, or her." He shook my hands vigorously, to punctuate his advice.

"Thank you. I'll do just that." The big Hau tree shadowed his face, but I knew how it looked and how it would always look to me, no matter what might happen to it in those insane races which were his life. "I'll begin now." He still had his strong grip on my hands and I leaned over them and kissed him, beginning softly, tempting him, teasing. And then he had pulled me hard against his body so that I felt every muscle, every ounce of sinew as if it were part of my own body, as if we were mated as I had known I wanted to be, almost the first time I saw him. And the teasing was over, and the softness. We were re-living those moments on the boat deck of the ship. His kiss was unexpectedly brutal, demanding, so intense it drained me of all strength. I was stirred as no emotion in my life had ever stirred me. . . . "Don't stop!" I wanted to say. "Go on forever. . . . And on. . . . Why must we stop with a kiss? There was nothing more tantalizing, more cruel than a kiss that could not further its intent.

Once, I had thought I knew love with Jacques Levescu. It was a childish game we had played, full of sexual,

106

athletic tricks, seeing how many ways of making love we could perfect. But this went so deep and searing, this small, unguarded moment between Luc and me, that I realized I had never grown up, never known sexual love until tonight.

It was Claire's light voice that tore us apart at last, I in haste, Luc slowly, letting go of my hands long after she must have seen us.

"Aren't you going to come and look at the outside of the place, Kay? Luc? Luc . . . you will like it. It will make you think of that chateau where we spent our honeymoon. What was it called, *mon cher?* I forget."

In French, he repeated, "You forget. You forget! I am sure you forget nothing!"

For the first time since I had known him, I thought Luc Sebastiani could be frightening. His low voice held a kind of controlled fury. I wondered if this was because he hated his wife very much, or because he loved her very much and resented her forgetting a memory vital to him. Because I was so jealous, so envious of her, I hoped, meanly, that he hated her. I wondered how many other women had shared him in adultery. And I hated them, too. Yet the one I should hate most was Luc, who led me on. . . . I'll show you, I thought in my frustration and bitterness. . . . I'll love any man I choose. I'll be as free as you. . . . And every man with whom I make love will be a club, a weapon against you!

So many drives of ambition seem to be sparked by a sex frustration, it is not surprising that I fell in love with that estate on that night and purchased *Makai* on my own behalf, under my own initiative. It took only two inspections by daylight to make the decision, although it did take several cables and two overseas calls to pound into Aunt Grace's head the idea that I knew what I was doing.

Whether it was Luc's departure almost immediately

107

with Claire for a month of golf and horseback riding on the Big Island, or merely Mother's quick recovery from a state of shock at the disclosure that I had bought *Makai* for my own use, I don't know, but I rushed around madly hiring men to handle redecorating, shoring up and repairing of my Island home, without once asking advice of either Mother or Aunt Grace.

"I don't think I've ever been so hurt," Mother had sobbed at first, explaining as she sopped up the tears with one of her exquisite old-fashioned lace handkerchiefs. "You know I wanted this for a honeymoon retreat. You must have inherited this selfish streak from your father's side of the family."

"Probably," I replied and went on measuring for new drapes in the master bedroom, whose entire south wall was of reinforced glass and presented a fabulous view of the Pacific horizon. Mike had volunteered to help me, and he laughed at my unthinking answer. It was after this episode, when Mother had shot her last arrow into the air and found it landed unnoticed, that she began to follow Mike's tactics. She became over-helpful, making a thousand suggestions which proved impractical but which I welcomed as I would always welcome signs of friendship from her.

Chiye Mitsushima, too, surprised me. Though she seemed to like me no better than ever, she had superb taste and a rare ability to coordinate colors, materials and furnishings. When *Makai* was ready for habitation again, Chiye took over the job as housekeeper, with the understanding that she hire a staff she found compatible, that she have my suite ready at a moment's notice, and that she stand guard—with guns, if necessary, to prevent the use of my suite by anyone else. Though, heaven knows, the biggest patio pool would be in constant use. Who would go into the warm, beautiful blue surf of Hawaii when they might dip into a very California pool? There were three of these, like the three bears, of diminishing size. Staring at me in her unblinking way, Chiye understood perfectly, and when it was presently broached by Mother that she and Mike borrow *Makai* for their honeymoon, it was Chiye who forbade them to use my own private rooms.

It was decided that Mother's marriage should take place the night before I sailed back to the Coast, and although I was sure Mike would not stick to it, he had superintended a legal agreement in which he made no claim whatever on Mother's money, or any that she acquired, beyond a life annuity to himself of fifteen thousand dollars a year. I was curious about the purpose of this, his adamant decision not to ask for more, in spite of the fact that I knew the fifteen thousand dollars per annum was not a Poverty Pocket. I also knew that, in his position, at that time, he could have asked for many times that figure and probably gotten it.

By the afternoon of the wedding, which was to be a civil service in the big living room of Mother's Waikiki suite, I had worked myself up to real enthusiasm. I found myself suggesting decorations, extra guests, my favorite champagne vintages, everything I hadn't experienced in my own Tijuana wedding. Mother thought it would be amusing if I were her Matron of Honor, and as I was the only attendant, I found myself in the position of giving the bride away. I did it with an odd lump in my throat. It was a pretty silly truth, but on the occasion of Mother's fifth marriage, I discovered I was sentimental.

The Sebastianis arrived from Hilo in time to drink a toast to the newlyweds before catching their own evening plane for the Coast. It had been five weeks since I last saw Luc, that night at Kahala, but there had never been a waking hour since that I hadn't re-lived those few stirring minutes, my mind and my senses erotically pursuing what must have followed in other circumstances, at an-

109

other time, the kind of lover he would make, the pulses he would excite, the positions he would know intimately . . . not smoothly. He would not be a smooth lover. I knew that now.

We all drank to the bride and groom, and then dozens of flash bulbs exploded and a half dozen newspapermen, both Occidental and Oriental, idiotically asked me, instead of the bride and groom, what were my views on the wedding. I found it harder and harder to answer stupid, impertinent questions with any degree of politeness. I had been doing this sort of thing now for six or seven years and, so far as I could see, the answers had never enlightened anyone. I was not witty, nor exciting copy. Only one thing about me was exciting, the fact that, thanks to some lack of chemistry between Mother and Father, I was an only child and therefore, quite possibly, the richest girl in the world.

During the evening whose noise, honeymoon sex jokes and forbidden thoughts of Luc were considerably blurred for me by champagne, I remembered that immediately after Mother and Mike left for their "secret" honeymoon base, Claire murmured quietly, "She's a remarkable creature, your mother."

Surprised, and with a prickle of uneasiness, I pretended a casualness I was far from feeling. "I think so."

Since I hadn't risen to the bait, she pursued the matter, a little less subtly. "It isn't every woman who would support poor Mike's—shall we call it—his past peccadillos?"

"Let's do call it that," I said as the champagne began to wear off. But, of course, I was dying of curiosity. Then Luc joined us, having served the last of the newspaper people and cleared them out.

"What is this all about." He asked sharply, glancing from his wife to me.

I said it was nothing, that we were talking about Mike's encumbrances, "such as they are," I ended. Although I

110

was called away to spell Mother's previous married names properly for the last reporter left jotting down some kind of code in the foyer, I heard Luc say to his wife in French, "It is no concern of yours. There has been a happy ending. Do not spoil it."

As may be imagined, this only whetted my curiosity, but I made an elaborate pretense not to care. Mother's young kitchen girl and the cleaning woman took care of the usual after-party confusion, and I left the deserted apartment with the Sebastianis. I was spending the last evening of that particular Hawaii visit in the suite I had rented on the floor below Mother's, but I took the elevator down with them to wish them a good flight that night. I knew it did me no good to be in Luc's company in this way, and I felt that he was aware of the same thoughts, but when Claire said in her bright way, "Come down with us, do, *chérie*," Luc added as I hesitated, "Please do come."

And of course I did. I couldn't help myself.

We said nothing in the elevator, either Luc or I. I remember thinking with a sick resentment and jealousy, "If he loves me, even a little, why must he remain with her? Is it only their religion that keeps them together, the fact that divorce is impossible to them? And then, the hideous, hurting answer: He still loves her. The thing that keeps them together is real love, transcending the physical, far beyond the little sensual titillation he felt —and so briefly!—for me."

It was this sense of loss, the sense of my having once again over-estimated a man's love for me, that spurred me on to buy and almost re-make my estate called *Makai*. It would spur me on, both to disaster and to pleasure earned, for many years ahead. I had learned early, as I thought, that love based on the senses only, was a delusion not worth the cost in anguish. From now on, I thought, my watchword would be: "I can afford it." If I

111

remembered this, I could never be disappointed in a man's motives.

We reached the lobby foyer and my depression was lifted by the amusing action of a photographer who yelled at us, "Here they come now!" I supposed, conceitedly enough, that the so-called Richest Girl in the World was the target. Instead, a newspaperman rushed out of the doorman's little office and signalled for a picture.

"I told you he was still here. Get him. The Grand Prix Winner. . . . The Cortot Team's Number One. . . ." As though Luc were a bullfighter or something. Claire Sebastiani was prepared though. Her frail, almost transparent hand went up to touch and adjust Luc's coat collar. He shrugged her hand off. I couldn't be sure it was accidental. But the picture the photographer got was a beauty, showing the Race Champion and his gorgeous, devoted wife. There was an unidentifiable figure in the background. Me! The fact that Claire had a perfect right to the conjugal pose didn't make me resent her less bitterly.

While the newsman was checking the correct spelling of the Corsican name "Sebastiani" with Luc, I said "bon voyage" to Claire and stepped back into the elevator. Claire glanced at Luc. I was sure she was wondering if Luc could overhear. Having decided, she said to me in a whispery voice, "I think we owe you this. Luc says it is no concern of ours, but I disagree. Your mother should know why Mike married her." She took a bent card from her evening bag, slipped it into my palm and hurried to join Luc. Just as he looked back at me, I pressed the elevator button.

I saw him look at me only a second or two across the full width of the foyer, but I knew that what I had read weeks ago in his gray-blue eyes, his steady gaze, was not a lie, and not a fleeting emotion. If Claire had hoped to promote something between us, for reasons of her own,

112

she had succeeded beyond her dreams. Playing it very light, I blew Luc a kiss and then he was lost to my sight as the elevator arose.

I looked at the card in my hand. The address was beyond downtown Honolulu, rather near the Bishop Museum. Otherwise, the card told me nothing. I made up my mind that nothing Claire Sebastiani did to disturb me was going to interfere tonight. It was simply her bitchy idea of causing trouble either for Mike or Mother or both.

All considered, I had a pleasant night's sleep, thanks to a couple of capsules and a sense that Mother ought to be out of my hair for at least a few months. At any rate, just to make sure, I would be sailing out of her reach tomorrow.

Just two hours before sailing the next day, however, my baser nature took over and I borrowed Mother's Porsche, which she seldom used, and drove into town and across to the address Claire had given me. I didn't know what I expected to find. No name was on the card. And when I reached the neat, little two-story apartment duplex within sight of the historic old museum, I found only two names on the mailboxes, a Miss Kay Tanaka, and a Mrs. Hizi Yamaguchi. It was a wild goose chase, an example of Claire Sebastiani's twisted sense of humor. But I rang the nearest bell, "Miss Tanaka," and a very pretty Japanese girl came to the door, yawning, in a wrinkled but beautifully patterned red and orange housecoat. She stretched and yawned again after looking me over.

"You want something, Miss? Make it fast. I've got to be on the job at four p.m."

"I'm sorry. I just wondered if the name 'Claire Sebastiani' meant anything to you. She sent me here."

"Never heard of her. Maybe it's the Yamaguchis you want. They live upstairs."

113

It seemed unlikely, but I ventured after a few seconds of thought, "Who are the Yamaguchis? A husband and wife?"

"No, no. An old lady and her grandson. Mickey. . . . That's the kid. He's real cute. Father's a *Haoli* boy. A big Irish looker. Works for some *Haoli* swell uptown."

"A big . . . Irish . . . looker?" The little square pegs began to fit into their little square holes. . . . "His name wouldn't be Mike Stannert?"

She shrugged. "Look, I really have got to get ready. Whyn't you go up and see the old lady? She's a nice old girl. She has a daughter works for some bigshots in Frisco. Maybe you know Chiye Mitsushima? It's her kid, this Mickey, that the old lady takes care of."

I leaned against the mail box and said quietly, "Yes, I know Chiye. Was she married to this Stannert?"

"You kidding? Then why's her name still Mitsushima? That was her husband. He's been dead for almost ten years, the old lady told me. The boy Mickey's eight or so. That tell you anything?"

TEN/

I HAD an hour and twenty minutes before the sailing, but infinitely more important, I had to make one of my most painful decisions in that time. While I was crawling into Mother's lowslung Porsche, the boy, Mickey Mitsushima, came out to join some neighboring boys. He was enchanting, with all his father's friendly Irish verve, combined with Chiye's smooth dignity and extraordinary presence. I envied Chiye, and I began to understand, or hoped I understood, exactly what Mike intended to do with the fifteen thousand dollars per year that was to be paid into that fund of his.

It was the sight of Mickey Mitsushima—or should it be Mickey Stannert really if not legally?—that made me decide not to tell Mother. One thing, however, seemed clear, and I decided to have that settled with Mike as soon as the right moment occurred. They would have to move to the Mainland, to California, or the East Coast, or even Mother's beloved, if somewhat tired French Riviera. Oahu was much too small to keep some busybody from telling Mother about the boy.

115

As I drove the car back to Mother's apartment and got a cab to the docks, I kept putting together bits and pieces of the Chiye-Mike relationship. Apparently, the boy, Mickey, was born before Chiye came to work for us in San Francisco. I wondered if it had been Chiye's idea to send Mike to work for Mother, with exactly this end result in mind, that if Mike could marry into a family like the Amberleys, Chiye's and Mike's child, and Chiye's mother, would always be secure. The revelation of the bastard child made Mike's actions despicable and yet oddly commendable in regard to that special trust fund he asked for. Chiye Mitsushima was another matter. Womanlike, I felt that she was the real betrayer. Never once had she hinted at this double life of hers. I was sure she must hate Mother and me fiercely, if she had to offer up her lover, her child's father, to sleep with another woman and to give another woman his name when the true Mrs. Mike Stannert ought to be Chiye herself.

Still, I left Hawaii that day without telling Mother, and without warning Mike that I knew. I felt that I was being forced to betray someone either way I turned, but Mother and I must have some similar reactions. Of all things in the world I hated most was the interference in my private life which was invariably prefaced by the hoary cliché: "I'm telling you this for your own good." I thought Mother would feel the same way. She would find out eventually. Meanwhile, I thought, a great deal depended on Mike's behavior to Mother.

The first night out was depressing. I kept remembering that other voyage, and Luc. I missed Luc so much I almost convinced myself I had a right to him, that Claire Sebastiani was the intruder. I began to analyze myself, find faults, a too-virginal, too-unchic attitude toward my life and the class of society into which I had fallen by an act of birth. In those days the Jet Setters were being

116

heard from more and more. I was still with those who literally enjoyed their travel. I still did stuffy things, and in all likelihood, Luc's wife whom he must prefer to all other women, was anything but stuffy. With my money she would, undoubtedly, have been a Jet Setter herself.

I missed Luc so much, and was so very much under the influence of a self-criticism binge that when I met a slim German movie actor, diffident and rather secretive, named Karl Dorn, I let myself be convinced he could be as necessary to me as Luc had been. On our third night out, after spending every waking hour in each other's company, we became lovers, partly because Karl seemed so desperately and cleanly in need of love. I discovered that in spite of his blond good looks, dramatic, sunken dark eyes, a hypersensitive mouth, and a voice that would eventually make him an international star, Karl was surprisingly inexperienced in affairs of the heart and body.

When I guessed his inexperience, I began to find an extraordinary delight in leading him to heights of feeling he obviously never dreamed of. He had begun to make love to me in dim lamplight on the carefully folded covers of my cabin bed and he exhausted his first craving by a rush at me like a pile-driver, which amused and even gave me a pleasure, beyond the pain of his amateurish assault. But I felt that he was worth something more than the brutish, animal act of copulation. While he lay there afterward, breathing deeply, weakened and sweating from his exertions, I began to work on each of the erogenous arcs of his body, to find the perfect key to his prolonged enjoyment of love. I was remembering always what I had been taught on that long-ago honeymoon with Jacques Levescu.

". . . . But that's sodomy," Ann Forrester had whispered, in horrified interest one time when we were discussing the ways to enjoyment of the human male. I had

117

laughed, but I often wondered if a simple word stood between Ann and her bull-necked Texas husband.

In a matter of minutes Karl Dorn was holding me tightly, muttering German words whose meaning I guessed, and behaving with more sophistication, satisfying us both, but unlike his first fumbling attempt, bringing us both to a climax of enjoyment in the beauty of the human body.

Afterward, Karl was transformed, his confidence in himself grown a little, but his dependence upon me in these areas I selfishly found irresistible.

He told me late one night when we had left my suite and were cooling off on deck, that he had exerted every effort in his life toward making a success in West Germany's burgeoning film industry. After the War's debacle had left him and his mother and older sister with nothing of the family's pre-War prosperity, his sister had supported the family. How, he did not say, except that his burning ambition had been to replace her as the breadwinner—and *Deutsch-marks*—winner of the family. I gathered without his saying so that his father and older relatives had been closely tied in with the Nazi Regime, but I didn't feel that it was my job to blame him for his father's sins. I rather admired him for having supplanted his sister as the moneymaker of the group. Although he was modest enough about his prowess as a lover, and with reason, he was frighteningly confident of his professional ability as an actor. This was a new reaction for me, and I thrived on it. I found that making my own decisions in love as in real estate, gave me a full and entire life for the first time in memory.

"In my profession, I am good," Karl repeated between his teeth, with all the stern, guttural dedication of a true German. "But really good."

I wanted to smile but didn't dare. Karl was one of those people one did not smile at, even when he and I were both in our twenties. In that regard he had scarcely changed several years later, except that all the "firmness" hardened him, not unsurprisingly, into the implacable perfectionist who is just one step from the psychiatrist's couch.

"Of course, you are good," I assured him with great enthusiasm. In spite of all the problems of this hypersensitive fellow, or quite possibly because of them, I found him intriguing and I could confess, to myself at any rate, that the two occasions on shipboard when we became lovers briefly were among my most satisfying memories. I could even begin to appreciate the thorough education I had received from Jacques Levescu. He may have been expensive, but—I could afford him!

In spite of my enthusiasm, Karl, in his usual overwrought way, complained, "You say these things, but you think of something else." I looked up, startled. It was never wise to underestimate an intelligence. "What were you thinking of then, darling Kay?"

I could have lied, but in my present state of self-confidence, I smiled instead and said with what I meant to be complete honesty, "I was thinking of my ex-husband."

Even in the moonlight, I thought he would slap me, he looked so affronted. . . . What a fool you are! I thought. . . . You take these little emotions much too seriously. . . .

He raised his voice, said he hated women who 'teased' and then, obviously curious, he added on a note of forced lightness, "Do I remind you of him? Never mind. I do not want to talk about him. Was I clumsy? Tomorrow, once we have docked, will I ever see you again?"

"Possibly. Who can tell? I haven't been to Europe since before my African job. Auntie is always threatening to make me go with her. She has a friend in Feldenstein she often visits." And the Sebastianis visited Feldenstein

119

too. I hadn't forgotten that. Some day they would return. There was a good track outside Feldenstein. The Cortot Team was sure to race there. And I might see Luc again. Love him again. . . . Be loved by him as only he knew how to make me love him.

Karl was mollified. The dangerously sensitive dark eyes softened and I was fully aware of his charm, which he seemed to do his best to hide beneath all this insistence upon how good an actor he was.

"Maybe we can meet closer to your home," he suggested. "I am expecting an offer from Hollywood." He said this in such a confiding ingenuous way I almost, but not quite, lost my usual suspicion. But if he was ingenuous, I no longer was.

. . . . Here it comes, I thought. . . . He wants to be close to the Amberley money, the Touch of Amberley. . . .

"I doubt it, Karl. I'll be in New York working on the Bastille Day Charity Ball, and then it's a group in Jamaica. I'm really very little known among the social dictators on the East Coast. I've never been on any 'best-dressed' or 'irresistible me' list, but I have some friends there. And they keep me busy, too."

He looked so disappointed I almost gave in and agreed to see him again while he remained in California, but something, it may have been my suspicious nature which seemed to have taken root, made me say, "Karl dear, I really would like to see you again, but believe me, you will be so busy you won't have time for any aftershipboard romances."

I kept to this note, how his great popularity would make any liaison with me impossible, and it worked well enough so that I was able to say a very amiable goodbye to him on the deck of the ship as we were coming into the old, familiar Pier 32.

"I will never forget this voyage," Karl promised me,

and looked as if he meant every word of it. I could almost believe him.

As he kissed me goodbye I remember thinking, "if this were only Luc!" and then feeling ashamed as I thought of all Karl Dorn's charm and intensity, his passionate dedication. . . . I was being unfair to him and I knew it. Some day, I told myself, we may meet again when I've forgotten Luc. Then my senses can do justice to the attractions of this intense fellow. Meanwhile, he is just too much!

I had scarcely reached the old, warm Victorian house where I lived with Aunt Grace before I was telling her all about the new me, though not, needless to say, about my conduct with Karl, or my feelings for Luc.

"I thought so," she remarked in her cynical, half-amused tone that I remembered so well. "I knew that the minute you started to complain about my renting the limousine that brought you home. All your talk about owning a 'decent' car! It's the influence of That Woman, I have no doubt."

I rightly applied *That Woman* to Mother, and assured Aunty that, if anything, Mother's influence on me was less pronounced than ever. "Except the way she spends money. In that way, I think she taught me a few things. But I'm tired of going through life missing things, just because we're Old Rich and not New Rich. If you ask me, the New Rich, gauche as they may be, have all the fun."

"I was afraid of that."

"Don't be miserly, Aunt Grace. Even with all the companies, corporations and charities, the government still has more fun with Amberley Money than I have. And I mean to change all that. I'm young, reasonably healthy. And somebody the other day called me beautiful—"

"Hmph," said Aunty, carefully blowing into each glove as she removed it. Her opinion of my "beauty" was

121

clearly not going to give me a superiority complex.

"He'd had a few drinks at the time. Anyway, with all this going for me, plus money. . . ."

"Especially money, My dear girl, I faced it long ago, and you may as well. A billionaire, especially a female billionaire, has one blinding radiant attraction. It is physically and mentally impossible for any other person in the entire world to look at your attractions, manifold as they may be, without being blinded by that one beacon-light. You are a billionaire."

"Okay. So I'll buy everyone." I went over to her lovely, old-fashioned three-mirror vanity table and, as she sat there on the little stool I'd once covered with some uneven petit point, I leaned over and put my cheek against hers. We looked at our reflection three ways, and liked what we saw. At least, we were thinking privately, it was not money that we saw in each other!

"I'm not saying anything is wrong with the way I was raised, Aunty. It's just that I'd like to live like other people my age, for a while. You know, be a glamorous, gorgeously dressed, fascinating and sexy post-debutante. A style-setter. A Jet Setter."

Aunt Grace laughed abruptly. She wasn't angry as I had expected her to be, though. "From all I hear, you can't be a member of the Jet Set and be sexy, too. That's the one thing they don't approve of. However, I see no way to stop you from making a fool of yourself. Everyone else in the family has done it."

"You're kidding! You too?"

"Me first!" she punned. She grinned into the mirror at our reflection. "I wasn't hard to take in those days."

I told her she wasn't hard to take now, which was true, but she made the perceptive remark that a woman in her sixties couldn't possibly know all the answers for a woman in her twenties.

"But when you've had your fling, Katy, you'll be back

to this dear old cave we live in. It's warm and homely and a refuge. Remember that." I said I would and she went on, thinking it over. "This may be for the best. What with my plans—"

"What plans?"

"Never you mind. But you need a modern image, for my plans. And you're quite right, Katy. You are entitled to show the world that those provincial San Francisco Amberleys can overshadow all the ridiculous creatures of that absurd little New York society world. And we can do it."

I hoped she was right, even though my self-confidence had not quite advanced to Aunt Grace's rarefied atmosphere where she could say: "We are the equal of all the rich in the world. And the superior of most, because we are richer than anyone else." It still seemed to me that there were thousands, probably millions throughout the world whose money was easier to use, easier to reach, less wrapped up in foolproof corporations, lands everywhere, under every city, and charities all over the world. My problem was that I could never forget my twenty dollar a week allowance which I received until my first marriage.

I was never afterward sure just when or how I became that better known Kay Amberley, the commodity called The Golden Kay of the Golden Gate, as some female reporter christened me on a day when there seemed no more worthy news of Jet Society. I reminded myself more and more of Mother, and I wondered if she would ever find out about Mike and Chiye, and if she would care. In the months that passed I heard no explosions from Hawaii, but I was exceedingly glad when Mike won a fabulous race in Mexico City and persuaded Mother to move there where he had been offered a substantial job in an industrial complex. What is more important, Mike persuaded Mother that it was more romantic to lease a pretty

123

middle-income apartment, than the penthouse of the swank Goya Palace.

Meanwhile, I didn't like the new Me very much and yet, once I was on the treadmill my pride, and my growing sense of Position in that world kept me on the treadmill. I thought the whole business discreditable, because I knew that the months I had spent in Africa, the summer vacations when I studied shorthand, typing and bookkeeping in our Amberley Pacific Shipping office, had made me a better person than I was now, when they began to call me "Golden Kay." The right shade of rinse on my hair helped to make the title, at least, legitimate. And one particular thirty thousand dollar charity donation, made with wide publicity, gave me a reputation for a great heart which far exceeded all the thanks the Amberleys had received in nearly a hundred years, despite the expenditure of countless millions for the benefit of mankind.

Aunt Grace merely grunted when I told her about this peculiarity of my new life. Very little surprised her. She even knew Karl Dorn.

"Not bad, that boy. He was one of the stars of the German film they had here at the Film Festival last year."

"And you went? Aunty!"

She grinned. "My German may be rusty but it's still competent enough for me to recognize good looks and pretty fair acting. I read the other day that he's in Hollywood now. So, he fell for you! I knew there was someone you met on that Hawaii jaunt, besides an old married man and Myra's Mickey Finn."

"An old married. . . . Oh, you mean Luc Sebastiani. Yes, I think I told you they attended the wedding."

"Must be a horror for Claire, being his wife."

I looked up sharply. "What do you mean? As a matter of fact, I'd say it was the reverse."

"That's a new one! Don't tell me Claire has taken up

racing! The near-misses Luc has had are more than I would bargain for in a husband."

So that was what she had meant! I didn't want to get involved in the subject of the Sebastianis. Aunt Grace was much too perceptive. But now that sufficient months had passed since what I secretly called "the great love of my life," I felt reasonably safe in discussing Luc.

"Do you really think he and Claire are happy? I mean, as man and wife?"

Aunt Grace saw no reason why not. "He adored her when they were married. I always suspected he was more fond of her than she was of him. He was famous, even then, you know. But if they aren't happy, they've had ten years to find out. Did you notice anything that suggested they weren't happy? Mind you, I don't mean ecstatic. Never saw a marriage that was ecstatic, after ten years."

I saw I was getting into deep waters, so I hastily swam out, with the disclaimer: "I don't know. I just wondered."

Nevertheless, I devoured all the sports pages and every magazine about racing. I flew down to Mexico City and over to Italy's Monza and several tracks in France, all ostensibly to organize some charity, or appear at a masquerade sponsored by the royal couple of Monaco, but I never met Luc. He was there. I watched him race. I had heart failure over a brief flameout once in Belgium, but I knew there would be no use in our meeting, or becoming lovers again. I finally convinced myself after nearly two years, that this long-distance infatuation of mine was ridiculous. And the brief occasions when I settled for second best with lovers I later despised, as I despised myself, taught me that though "Golden Kay" might rate high on the dubious lists of International Society, she rated a big goose egg as a human being. If I hadn't thought so myself, my school friend, Ann Forrester Haight would have let me see subtly enough in her case, less subtly in the case of her husband, Morgan. I hadn't liked him from the start, and his disapproval of me now was insultingly clear.

"Guess who I'm bringing up to dinner," Aunt Grace announced when she called me at my Imperial Towers penthouse out on Taylor Street with a view of the Golden Gate and half of Marin County.

"Not Mother and Mike. They flew up from Acapulco this afternoon. They're staying at the Mark Hopkins. I expect them about six."

"Still together, eh? No. I'm not bringing them. Wait 'til you see. It's someone you liked, someone you liked very much, and who adores you."

Luc! Who else was also a friend of Aunty's? Luc, and Claire, of course. There would always be Claire. I rushed around changing my new hostess pajamas a dozen times, changing my jewelry and my hairdo, making my hair a mess, each time calling in Tetsu, my cook and houseboy, and Pegeen, my maid, to give me their solemn opinion. They had both been drilled to perfection in their jobs by Aunt Grace's competent master-sergeant, Hildy. I knew by now that small, charming, diplomatic Tetsu would manage to please me each time I called on him to do so, but he salved my vanity, and I was going through a phase when I liked myself less and less. This was just before the Pucci revolution in color, and I kept worrying for fear Luc's, and especially Claire's French taste would despise the brightness of my outfit. I finally gave up the fight for a special look and with the help of Pegeen who was young and Irish and enthusiastic, I got myself recombed, brushed and properly made up to look unmade-up. I was still nervous when we heard the buzzer and Tetsu answered the house phone from the doorman. Pegeen clapped her hands and announced happily, "Sure, it's himself is here."

"Which himself is this?" I asked as Tetsu told the

126

doorman to send them up, whoever "they" were. But my heart was stilling me all the same. "Run and check the canapes," I said much too briskly. "Those damned catered canapes are never as good as the ones Tetsu prepares."

"If you'll be taking my word, M'am, they're that delicious I could've ate 'em all."

I had a feeling Tetsu would find there was a distinct shortage of canapes but the dinner would be excellent, and just the thing to keep Mother in a good humor, because no one else could prepare Tempura and the whole Japanese menu quite as well as Tetsu could. Besides, if I could just get over this idiotic teen-age crush routine, with its ever recurring thoughts of Luc Sebastiani, I could at least enjoy the usual excitement that guests showed over the apartment. I had owned it for about a year and a half, but I never stopped enjoying it, as well as the awed reactions of my guests. I was learning that there were many sensations to be enjoyed by one who was rich, even if one had the bad taste to flaunt them.

And then Tetsu passed us on his way to the foyer. I hurried after him. Tetsu opened the door and I saw first that noble, disapproving Texan, Morgan Haight, who looked exactly as he had ten years before, disapproving. He and Ann had been away for six months, at his family home in a suburb of Dallas for the birth of their second son. Morgan had wanted boys, and, as Ann remarked to me laughingly before they left, "I won't dare have a female until Morgan approves."

Ann rushed past him and we hugged each other and I said she was looking marvelous, but she denied this with an angry shake of my shoulders.

"Fat and matronly, you mean. I've gained eight pounds since Arthur was born."

"We shouldn't have come tonight," Morgan said stiffly, hesitating before Pegeen took his coat. "You are having company."

127

"Only people you know. Mother and her husband. Mike is very nice. And Aunt Grace. She is bringing. . . ." Morgan and Ann were discussing whether they should stay, and I didn't finish explaining. Somehow, if I began to discuss Luc and Claire with them, I felt that Ann's sharp senses and Morgan's sharp eyes would chop away all my defenses and guess the truth.

But when the Haights had been persuaded to remain, Pegeen settled them down to drinks and *hors d'oeuvres* at the long Mediterranean buffet by the French doors that opened onto the terrace. It was a clear but starless night with surprisingly little fog, and I thought of Hawaii. Strange that in spite of my feelings for Luc, which persisted so maddeningly, all the delicate, unbelievable sensations of ecstasy I had known with him on deck that night were blurred into an indistinct composite. I could not sort them out any more.

There were sounds, women's voices, in the foyer, and I hurried back through the apartment, then abruptly slowed my pace, knowing Aunt Grace would see more anxiety in me than I wanted her to see. Aunt Grace and Mother had both arrived at the same time with their entourage, though not including the pair I expected. Mike was there, being gallant but not ostentatious, with Mother. He had acquired an air of quiet authority that seemed to have a good effect on Mother and I assumed, from their reactions to each other, that the Chiye episode and Mike's child were matters still unknown to Mother. I felt things might be reasonably safe, so long as they didn't return to Hawaii.

Behind them, however, came Aunt Grace and her guests. I caught sight of the dark blond hair of a male of middle height and knew that I had guessed wrong. Instead of Luc and Claire Sebastiani, she had brought Karl Dorn, my young German lover of my return voyage two years before, and with him was a black-haired actress

128

from Eastern Europe, notable for her off-screen appearances in the company of the very rich, males preferably. I knew I would be expected to recognize her and fortunately, just as I reached the group, her name, Lisa Kestner, came to me. Apparently, she was Karl's date tonight.

"You needn't worry," I thought, reading the challenge direct in the dark actress' eyes. "I've no intention of trying to snatch your boyfriend away from you."

However, like most women of a similar age, thrown in each other's company, Miss Kestner and I treated each other first with extra-politeness and later with the free and easy, slightly feline friendship that is demonstrated at its best when two feminine rivals lock arms at a night club and visit the Powder Room together. As for Karl, since I had hardly given him a thought after discussing his movie career with Aunty nearly two years ago, I was surprised at his attitude toward me. He acted as though he still felt something of that infatuation which had occupied us both on shipboard.

"I was afraid they would have spoiled you by now, but they have not. You are so like the fairy princess," he said as he kissed my hand. Then, to my surprise and certainly that of my other guests, he kissed me on the lips, hurried and determined, like a lover taking his prerogatives and not sure of his reception. Immediately, he backed off, a bit flushed, as he noticed the attention he caused, and I didn't have a chance to give him a very feeling return before Mother asked archly, "Well, well, how long has this been going on?" and Morgan Haight, coming out of the dining room with a bourbon highball, looked on the scene with characteristic disdain. It was the sight of Morgan, I think, whose influence on Ann was so dampening, that made me play up to Karl.

As often happens in life, when you "play up," the performance gradually turns to reality. His accent was not

129

much improved, but it added just the dash of glamor that his intensity required. And then too, though he seemed exceedingly sure of himself as an actor—Aunty said he had won several international awards lately—I sensed that he still had the endearingly young, bullish, yet uncertain approach to love, which was absurd because I was by no means as uncertain as he seemed to be of his sex appeal.

While we all buzzed around the buffet and the bar, Karl threw open the terrace doors with one of those nervous movements I silently dubbed Master Race Gestures, and he began to inhale the crisp San Francisco night air.

"Marvelous, this air! I envy you. It makes one want to —do great things."

"Like conquer the world?" I asked, but Karl didn't see either the humor or the irony of my remark.

Since it is nearly impossible in my native town to have air without either wind or fog, the others of my guests were almost blown away and Morgan rushed over to close the doors, while Karl looked from the big Texan to me, so perplexed I had to laugh at his expression.

"We haven't all got your iron constitution," I explained, although he did not look nearly as toughened and leathery as Morgan Haight, or Mike Stannert. Since I could see that Karl's friend, Lisa, was behaving toward Mother with determined charm, and Aunt Grace was having a pleasant gossip between Ann and Mike, I let myself be drawn out onto the terrace by Karl Dorn. He was looking particularly attractive, his dark eyes lighted and bright against the healthy Nordic pallor of his face and tawny hair. He was still trim to the point of being meagre and I suspected his success kept him keyed up. He looked back, saw we were alone, and said, "You weren't here two months ago. I cut out during shooting to fly up and see you."

"No," I said, thinking back. "I was at Gstaad. Skiing."

"I came up last Christmas but even your Aunt was gone."

"We spent the holidays with Aunty's cousins in Virginia."

"Lisa says she saw you at the Monza Grand Prix. I didn't know you went in for that sort of bloody business."

He had always seemed to me so much on the razor edge of violence that this surprised me.

"I have friends who race." I glanced back at Mike who was laughing at one of Aunt Grace's dry, witty remarks.

"Friends, not lovers. Don't say lovers," he repeated and looked at me. His sincerity may have been admirable, but it made me uneasy. He had apparently never played the game without becoming serious. I hoped he would not become boring as well. He took both my hands before I could move and play down this mood of his. "You think I am joking. But I am not. I thought I would forget what we were to each other on shipboard. There have been other women. I am very popular, you know."

I couldn't help smiling, though I made it as tender a smile as possible. "I am sure of it. You are popular with me."

"Good." He grinned with one of his quick changes of mood. "Because I knew then that as soon as my salary was respectable, I would marry you."

"Remarkable! You knew two years ago?"

"It was only a matter of waiting until you were lonely enough and I was rich enough. Only—" He shrugged and shook my wrists lightly, "You betrayed me. You became more popular. And further away then ever. But now, you are here, and I am here, and it is fate. We should take advantage of fate. Think how long it may be before fate brings us together again so carefully."

131

This time I laughed so hard my other guests stopped drinking and talking to look out at us through the glass doors. He glanced their way too, but undisturbed.

"Shall we begin by getting acquainted again?"

I agreed gravely. "All marriages should begin with at least an hour or so of acquaintance."

He kissed me, and this time, in spite of the chill of the evening, I was astonished at the depth of my own response. And all the time we kissed, I remember thinking with a cruelty I could not seem to prevent, "Maybe he could blot out Luc from my thoughts, my dreams. This hot, bodily craving for Luc would weaken and vanish. Why not, if the proper legal steps are taken to prevent Karl's getting his hands on the Amberley money? All his talk about making a respectable salary is . . . talk. To impress me. But that doesn't matter. After all, I can afford him."

ELEVEN/

KARL'S JOKE, which is how I regarded his proposal, was a pretty poor basis on which to build a marriage, but as his persistence and undeniable charm wore me down, I found myself taking him more seriously, until I gave in for many reasons. Aunt Grace, surprisingly, made no objections. It was Mother who told me with the sweet, patronizing voice of the happily married, "You must be very very sure, dear. As sure as I am of my boy. There must be no one else in your life. Any more than there is in Mike's or mine."

In a single moment of premonition, I shivered at her words. I could never forget the two who would always be in Mike's life—his ex-mistress, Chiye, and their son.

There were minutes between Karl and me so intense, when he seemed to need me so much, that I often suspected I was subconsciously making Karl pay for my own thwarted love affairs with Luc and with Jacques Levescu. Even so, I hesitated before marrying Karl, and went so far as to postpone our wedding day, an act which he pointed out would be sure to bring bad luck. Karl was more than a little superstitious.

"We will fly to my Rhineland home for the ceremony," Karl announced enthusiastically. "And no cameras. No reporters. Only you and me." He took my hands in that boyish gesture of his which was so endearing, and he added, "You are fortunate. No . . . what you call in-laws. I am alone in the world, but for you, my angel."

I was at least perceptive enough to appreciate his sincerity and the fact that he obviously loved me more than I loved him. "Maybe this is the secret of a happy marriage for me . . . to be loved, rather than 'in love,' " I thought. Nevertheless, I explained that it would hurt everyone too much if I ran away from my own people, to be married in a foreign country.

"I hurt everyone very much when I did that before."

Karl took his hands off me quickly. His face looked white and strained and vulnerable.

"Don't! I don't want to hear about the others." He got hold of himself, probably because I looked so startled. "I am sorry. You see, on the pretty white ship that time, I wondered how many there had been before me."

"Not many. In fact—"

He kissed me and never learned that up to the moment we met, my most thorough indoctrination had come with my first husband. It was, though I didn't point it out to Karl, that very indoctrination by Jacques which made me capable of giving Karl such ecstatic pleasure. I thought there was no need to confess that my experience since our shipboard encounter, while selective, was much fuller than he would have liked.

"But that's a man for you," I told Mother, who had come up from Mexico to see what my wedding plans actually were, and whether I was being wise in withholding Karl's rights on any property or money of mine.

134

"How do you mean, Kay? Not but what any generality about a man is certainly true."

I explained while considering the half dozen possible cocktail suits sent over for me to make my choice for the wedding.

"Because a man wants you to be good in bed, but he doesn't want you to have learned your skill from anyone."

Mother surprised me by looking affronted, but Aunt Grace, who had come into hear this last remark of mine, laughed abruptly.

"Just be careful what teachers you employ, Katy, in any field. I must say, I had someone else picked out for you, but this boy isn't bad, really. *If* you can put up with the Hollywood entourage that is sure to follow him around."

This hadn't occurred to me, and I assured everyone I wasn't going to live in Hollywood where we would be a constant target for cheap publicity and all the gimcracks that went with Karl's new American fame. He seemed strangely unaffected by it, so far, but I was sure that before long, he would find it all as entrancing and necessary as most actors found it. I didn't quite know how this would affect me, but by that time, surely Karl would see that he need not count so much on his career. We could certainly live on my money. There was no sense in his being tied down by those silly films to which he seemed to give his heart's blood.

"Tell me, Katy," Aunt Grace said suddenly as I explained something of my views to her, "Why are you marrying that nice fellow?"

A little irked, I reminded her, "He's not a boy, though you act as though I were taking advantage of him. He is as old as I am. And he knows what he is doing. However, I don't mind telling you that when I am with Karl,

135

I feel wanted. I feel necessary to someone. . . . What do you say to this cloth of gold suit?"

"Pretty obvious; isn't it, dear?" Mother remarked. She looked so self-satisfied, I envied her. She was right about the cloth of gold suit. I finally chose the elegantly simple richness of the Dior import and was still thinking about Mother's better-late-than-never happiness when she got up to go and meet Mike. "We've had to let our Mexican housekeeper go. She got pregnant; wouldn't you know? I thought it would be a darling thing, Kay, if you'd give me that Japanese woman to get things running smoothly. The one in charge of *Makai*."

I dropped the hanger and apologized to the woman from the shop as we both picked up the suit skirt, while I wondered what excuse I could make to keep Chiye away from Mother and Mike. As I hesitated, Aunt Grace's eyebrows knit. Clearly, she found something odd about my long pause. Mother chose to assume the worst, that I didn't want to part with the woman. I made an excuse that no one knew *Makai* as well as Chiye did, and then asked, "What does Mike say? Does he also insist on having Chiye as housekeeper?"

Mother hadn't bothered to ask Mike, and I made some sort of non-commital promise. After she had gone, Aunt Grace said to me, her clever gaze troublesome, "Since when are you so fond of Chiye?"

I changed the subject as Karl had just arrived after flying up from a full day of shooting in Hollywood and we wanted to discuss our honeymoon plans. He wanted to know if all the plans had been worked out for the ceremony at the local Lutheran Church.

"I don't mind telling you, Kay," Aunty put in, "that it ought to be Methodist-Episcopalian, the way all the Amberley brides were married. We are lucky that the Reverend Dr. Benstrom knew all the details of your first wedding. A regular marriage and divorce would have put a serious crimp in your plans."

So we all got off the subject of Chiye which made me so uneasy. Sometimes during the hectic days before the wedding. I felt that the whole thing was one of those nightmares which are half reality and half horror. I kept telling myself how devastating it must be to marry and share a lifetime with a man who adored me much more than I loved him. I could simply be kind, and be rewarded by the love of this decent, passionate fellow for me. I wouldn't make the mistake that Jacques and, in a way, Luc, had made, of disdaining the love I offered. "It is better to be loved than to love," I told myself again. I was still repeating this secretly during the moments of the actual wedding ceremony. Mother and Aunt Grace and Ann and Morgan Haight were witnesses. None of us wanted publicity, and yet, when Karl and I left the church after the cold, austere Lutheran wedding service, I was amazed to see at least two dozen milling, noisy people, mostly teen-agers, who ran toward us as we got into Karl's Mercedes-Benz.

"Karl. . . . Oh, Mr. Dorn! Can I have your autograph?" The refrain was repeated endlessly.

Feeling like a dog in the Manger, I disliked Karl's fans and I have a suspicion I was jealous of their interest in him. I wanted to belong to Karl and to have Karl belong to me. I felt that I was done with loving a man more than he loved me. I didn't want to divide Karl with thousands of screaming, impassioned girls who didn't even know him.

"They are calling you," I said, but he looked agitated, almost angry, and answered harshly, "Do not look at them. Darling Kay, you have not thrown the little bouquet."

The tiny sprig of muguet was about the size of a pomander ball and I reached out the car window, seeing our wedding party wave to us. At the same time Karl's fans started to run across the church parking lot between our car and the family. So I made one heroic gesture and hurled my little muguet over the heads of the shrieking girls, hoping to get it to Aunty or Mother. As luck would have it, one of the long-legged girls gave a gigantic leap, grabbed the bouquet, and as Karl drove out of the lot, I saw the delicate white and green flowers torn to pieces among his fans.

We flew to Germany that night to please Karl who wanted to show me his home on the Rhine, but I felt curiously flat, depressed. Not that I liked my new husband less, but because, in this wedding I had felt none of the walking-on-clouds magic of my first breathtaking marriage. How odd, and significant, that Luc had seen Jacques and me at our Mexican wedding supper! Would Luc always overshadow my life and happiness?

I smiled a great deal at Karl on the flight over the Pole, but my teeth felt as though they would be chattering any minute, and I was beginning to come out of the anesthesia of the wedding, to realize how little I had wanted to take this serious step in my life.

We touched down at Frankfurt and took a local plane to Karl's town on the Rhine. By this time, what with the leaps and jumps of time, we were in no mood for the huge, screaming crowd that met us in Klagenfurt.

"*Bitte*," said the German stewardess, "If the Herr Dorn will allow—we let the other passengers disembark, and the Herr Dorn may exit with the crew."

It was astounding that this frightful, yelling mob predominantly of females, was actually here to get an autograph from their hero. Not that Karl's performances, his ability and looks didn't deserve the attention, I told myself at once, but he never seemed aware of his own popularity, and it was hard for me to comprehend the full extent of it.

Feeling like a slave who must make way for her master, I came down off the plane alone, trying hard, for Karl's sake, to smile. It did seem amusing, though, when reporters and photographers who had always upset me with their attentions, now rushed madly past me, one of them spinning me around as he passed, in order to get pictures of the New Germany's most famous international star. And I was proud for Karl, proud, too, that he loved me. He was being rushed through the gauntlet now, assisted by two chic German stewardesses, and he waved his hand before his eyes, ruining several flashshots. He was looking around, seeking a face in the crowd, and it seemed strange, but endearing that the face he sought was my own.

I was just about to move out into the little circle of excitement when a voice spoke to me, sleek, faintly accented, evoking a thousand memories that degraded and humiliated me.

"A happy meeting, ma petite! You have grown to a real beauty since . . . Tijuana."

Just as Karl saw me and came to join me, drawing with him the attention of the crowd, I looked over my shoulder and into the sickeningly familiar face of Jacques Levescu. He was smiling, his special, pleasing smile, which, as I remembered its use, indicated that he wanted something. He seemed no different from the man I had known and idolized a dozen years before, and yet, the very fact that he had not changed gave him a seedy look, like a garment styled ten years ago and looking unused but no longer new.

I said coolly, "Hello, Jacques. Have you been behaving yourself?"

"*Comme-ce, comme-ça.* I have missed my little girl."

139

He grinned more widely. It was strange to see him standing there looking so much as he had looked in the old days, the days of our honeymoon, and yet to feel nothing for him, not even hatred. In some ways, I knew, he had been good for me. In other ways, by putting a price tag on love, he had set the pattern for my future. It was too late now to call back my ideas of life, the bitter panacea I had worked out for all actions of mine: "I can afford it. . . ."

Karl strode up to take my arm now, pulling me close to him possessively, as he gave Jacques a polite though puzzled smile.

Following Karl's lead, I put my arm around him as well, so that we presented a united front to all intruders. "Darling," I said to Karl, "this is Mr. Levescu. I was once married to him for a short time."

I had tried to make the introduction as innocuous as possible, for Karl's sake, knowing how jealous he was of my past, but naturally, Jacques took advantage of the moment, guessing by Karl's suddenly rigid face, how badly this news hit him. Jacques held out his hand while Karl hesitated, trying to get hold of himself, and his emotions which appeared to me to be forever exposed.

"It all seems a very long time ago; doesn't it?" I asked brightly, seeing that Karl hadn't found anything to say, but I could feel all his muscles stiffen close against my body.

"Not to me," the detestable Jacques contradicted me. "It might have been yesterday. I have forgotten nothing about my enchanting little bride."

Karl flushed darkly and clenched his fist just as a news photographer exploded a flashbulb in our faces. I could already imagine the caption on that picture tomorrow. I said quickly, "Hadn't we better get out of this crowd, darling?" And I added deliberately, "After all, this is our honeymoon."

140

This reminder seemed to have a good effect on Karl, and he began to move away with me, whereas, Jacques stood there staring at us, his smile too fixed to be natural.

"Where to now?" I reminded Karl who had almost walked us into another cameraman. Karl ducked and scowled as the flash went off in his face, but we kept going. As for me, I had learned in the last few years how to roll with the punches, how to present at all times a blank but smiling countenance to the camera. Karl was too sensitive ever to be as completely prepared as I was.

Fortunately for Karl's temper, some of his fans and a couple of reporters got between us and the insufferable Jacques.

We got a taxi and were driven to a charming, newly rebuilt little hotel with a distant view of the green, curving Rhine that flowed past the town. A studio friend of Karl's had reserved our suite under another name and there were no crowds to greet us, not even, I was happy to see, a photographer. From the way Karl looked around the cozy lobby with its open fireplace very black, and its worn but comfortable overstuffed chairs, I guessed that the house meant even more to him than a place for a honeymoon.

"Was this once your home?" I guessed, and he nodded.

"Most of it was destroyed late in the War, about the time of the Remagen Bridge. I was a boy then, and I remember how frightened I was of the big Yanks, as we called your people. And in the end," he had glanced around and then his gaze fixed on me with that very young and slightly sad smile, "In the end, you see, we are united, you and I. The Yank and the Rhinelander."

"Darling," I reminded him, guessing what was in his mind from his tension, "If we don't hurry, we won't have very much time to unite. A week isn't a very long honeymoon."

He hurried me up the narrow, twisting and turning

141

staircase to our third floor suite with its enchanting dormer windows close under the low roof.

"Hurry!" he commanded, beginning to fumble with the emerald clasp on my sables. Tired as I was after our nightlong flight across half the world, I was touched and even aroused by his enthusiasm, his energy. The very fact of our having met Jacques, and his snide hints to my new husband, gave me the sensual stimulus I needed to take fire at my husband's touch, and to bring him up, as he brought me, to a fine, hair-trigger pitch of enjoyment.

It was a huge, deep bed with a fabulous mattress, and it seemed to enclose us in its warmth, even as my own affection enclosed my husband in its protective sheath. For those minutes, prolonged to hours, at least, we were completely happy. Curiously enough, I was content in the knowledge that I had made my husband happy, and that we were in this old-fashioned, inexpensive hotel room, once a private bedroom, for our love, our pleasure. I forgot just for a little while, the title Jacques Levescu had first sounded in my ear: The Richest Girl in the World. Because this happiness of mine in being wanted did not depend upon my money, but upon my body, and its skill, its pitch to the highest key of sensuous enjoyment.

We ordered our meals in our room and sat together at the window later, with Karl's arm around me, while he described his childhood and wondered what I had been doing at those times.

"I read about you, once," he said after a while, thoughtfully. "There were the shortages and the Black Market and my sister with the G.I.s, getting Mother and me enough to eat, and then I read about this girl in America who had so many clothes that each time she changed, for a meal, or to be driven to school, she had to choose from a great catalogue of her clothing, a catalogue whose pages

142

were changed almost weekly. 'The Richest Girl in the World.' That is what the article called you. It seemed very strange. Very thrilling."

"How horrible for you, when you and your family were suffering! Anyway," I added, "it wasn't true about the catalogue of clothes. That happened to Mother when she was a girl. They simply made it up about me."

But all beautiful things come to an end, and our little idyl was over all too soon. Karl's American studio had sent its German representatives to interview us and get —of all the impertinence!—honeymoon shots of us! I asked Karl not to reply to the demands and, in fact, to treat the reporters with the indifference I customarily used, but Karl insisted that he owed it to the studios which had spent so many millions grooming and building him. I didn't see it at all, but because Karl wished me to, I went along with it, secretly determined not to have it happen again. Karl would have to learn that we were not to be used for publicity in this way. Nevertheless, even to help Karl, I found it all embarrassing and out of place. Nor did it make me any happier to read Jacques Levescu's comments in a column under his own byline:

"WHAT IT'S LIKE, LIVING WITH THE RICHEST GIRL IN THE WORLD"

This column had been placed deliberately beside the flash picture of Karl and me at the airport, with me surprised, Karl frowning and Jacques Levescu, on my other side, dominating the scene with his broad, self-satisfied smile.

I had only just started to read the interview under Jacques' byline as I stood waiting in the lobby for Karl to buy pipe tobacco when Karl joined me.

"What is it, darling? You look like a thundercloud."

"Nothing," I said hastily, having read enough to guess at Karl's violent reaction. But he was already reading:

". . . incredibly inexperienced little virgin I was fortunate enough to initiate into the mysteries of life and sensuous worlds of . . ."

"It was that oily devil who taught you! That cheap, Continental gigolo! I'll kill him!"

"No, you won't. Now, listen to me." I tried very hard to make him see reason, but I was nearly as furious at Jacques as he was. "He's done this purposely to ruin things for us. He will keep on until we pay him off. I know his type."

"Pay him off! I'll pay him off with a bullet, this blackmailing—"

The receptionist was looking at us, and so was an efficient, straight-haired young German woman in a severely tailored suit. I suspected she might be a reporter, and Karl's reaction would be perfect fodder for a followup to Jacques' story. Because Karl refused to "hide out" any longer, as he put it, we ate in the local Kursaal that night, to the accompaniment of the Wedding Song played with gusto by violin, piano and cello as we entered the dining room. This, of course, did not make us any less conspicuous, but I hoped for the best. We almost made it without a scandal, but halfway through the excellent *sauerbraten mit spatzle*, I became aware of someone coming up behind my chair, and from the sudden, angry look on Karl's face, I guessed it was Jacques. Hoping vainly to avert the threatened trouble, I put my hand out to touch Karl's fingers in both warning and trust. At the same time, Jacques leaned over me and kissed me on the nose as, suspecting his gesture suddenly, I started to move my head.

After that, everything happened at once. Karl got up so quickly his chair skittered across the floor, and before Jacques could make his expected syrupy remark, Karl's

144

fist caught him on the chin and throat. Then my ex-husband was lying in an awkward bundle on the floor, half propped against the leg of a neighboring table.

My honeymoon with Karl was over almost before it began. We were on every trashy entertainment page in the world, or so it seemed.

TWELVE/

I suppose it was inevitable that our marriage should fail, since my own approach to it had been nearly as juvenile as Karl's, with his insecurity and the quick temper that was touched off by any threat to his self-esteem or his "property." This same quick temper could be turned on me as easily as upon those outsiders who threatened his happiness, but the greatest pity of all was that any faults of his hadn't the power to hurt me, or make me adapt my own faults to please him. I had gone into the marriage without love, although I felt for him an affection and unquestionably enjoyed being with him, pleasing him. Worst of all, I had liked his emotional dependence on me. Hardly a quality to ensure a successful marriage. I couldn't very well explain this to Aunt Grace, however, and I merely fumbled for excuses when her letters repeatedly asked when we were going to start a family for her to rear "and spoil as I spoiled you."

Our entire visit to Europe was one long series of disastrous public encounters. Jacques Levescu did not pursue us beyond Germany, and I learned later that he had found a new heiress while haunting the Feldenstein Casino, which caused Karl and me to pass up Aunt Grace's cabled suggestion that we stop in and see her friend Princess Sophie-Frederick.

When Karl and I were in Berlin, I read of the "engagement of distinguished diplomat Jacques Levescu to Matilde Marlene Shrieber, the only daughter of West Germany's newest billionaire."

"Poor Matilde Marlene," I remarked before I thought.

Karl was tearing up his copy of the paper and at my words, he muttered, "Must that creature be with us forever?"

I tried to soothe him but, of course, it was no use.

"Darling, he hopes we'll be annoyed. He lived on such annoyance. Probably considers his discretion is worth money."

"If you again suggest bribing him, I swear I will—"

"For Heaven's sake, lower your voice and calm down!"

Then I changed the subject, without much effect. Karl's constant raw nerves were a little more than I had bargained for, and much too early in our marriage, they became less and less endearing, more troublesome.

In Paris, Karl's studio sent a handsome young male fan magazine writer to interview us, and when the writer asked if I had been married before, though he obviously knew the answer, Karl assumed he was being sarcastic, and went off on a tirade about the stupidity of the press. He ended by demanding to know what a gigolo like Levescu had to do with the career of one Karl Dorn. I wasn't too surprised when the Frenchman slanted the article to emphasize Karl's "Teutonic Temperament" which automatically cost him thousands of French fans with long war memories.

But Karl and I were unquestionably married, and I had for him a very real affection amounting at moments to love. I tried to interest him in some of the overseas charities, the schools for modern manual training, the children's training centers established by Amberley endowments, but Karl was an actor first, last and always, and like many another talented egotist, he had but one interest in life. There was a stubborn honesty about this which I admired even after I, an egotist also, began to find it hard to shape my entire life and conduct with the sole end of keeping Karl from becoming upset.

Karl was called back to Hollywood shortly after the Paris interview episode, when he was nominated for an Academy Award for his really remarkable performance in "Mad Winter." I returned with him, direct to Los Angeles, without even a chance to see my family. I explained long distance to San Francisco and Aunty who understood and encouraged me in my efforts to "make myself a good wife" as I put it hopefully. Mother and Mike seemed in a status quo, down in Acapulco, although the Chiye Mitsushima matter was still in abeyance.

Karl was convinced that I could find more "to occupy you" as he put it, in Hollywood than in San Francisco, and I felt he deserved the chance to prove it.

If we were to make a go of this marriage, we ought to start a family before we both became too immersed in other and outside matters and drifted on into the indifference I saw in other relationships where there were no children. But when I broached the subject, Karl was evasive, putting off even a discussion of children and I began to wonder if my mental image of two boys near the same age, and then a sister for them a little younger, would ever come to fruition. I started to be even less fussy: "I'll take anything I can get," I said, jokingly, in a letter to Aunty. "Say—two girls with or without the boy. But I wouldn't like there to be an only child. Only children can get pretty lonely. And spoiled, too," I reminded her. It was all just talk, though, so far. And Karl was

148

never so drunk with passion and desire that he forgot about caution.

One day he came driving out Wilshire to our hotel apartment full of vim and vigor, claiming the desire for me suddenly overcame him. Also, he was not shooting his scenes until night, and, as he put it, "I want to have something to think about during the long, dark hours ahead." Half playfully, but with that strength I had learned to respect, he pushed me toward his bedroom with its big, over-sized furniture that looked to me heavily Germanic. He was undressing me hurriedly, all thumbs with my zipper, and grateful aloud that I wasn't wearing a girdle. Before I could move to the big bed, he threw me backward upon the bed, covers and all, and leaped onto me with a smothering jolt that made me groan and laugh at the same time. There was always something very young and impulsive about him that would be endearing to any woman of sufficient stamina to receive him every time he behaved like this.

I discovered at once, however, that during those long hours at the studio, someone had given his lovemaking a finesse it had not possessed before. His natural drive and aggression were certainly channelled now to a gentleness of the hands and teasing fingers upon my breasts, my abdomen, working toward my thighs. I was also able to reach a climax so stimulating it made every nerve in my body come alive with the exquisite pain that caused me to love Karl for the first time as I loved Luc Sebastiani. I saw Karl suddenly as Aunt had said before our marriage, "too good for me," the kind of man who could help me to be a good wife and mother. Our future would not be the barren thing my life had been up until now.

Like most women, I broached the subject at a time when Karl, lying beside me, was still in the throes of

149

pleasant exhaustion and my breaking into his sensual aura disturbed him. He raised up on one elbow and stared at me, his pale German blue eyes alarmed.

"Kay! We must not. Only yesterday my agent warned me. There must be no children yet. The Image, it will be so bad with the young . . . people . . . who worship me."

"Young girls, you mean." I moved my head to face him. Just as I had killed his mood, he had shattered mine. He saw how hurt I was and went on quickly, stammering a little as he did when he was nervous.

"I'm sure my darling would not think of conceiving a life at the time when we need no intruders, no one else to enter our lives." To soothe me, he reached over and began to run his hand along my flank with great care and sleepy, voluptuous movements.

But his choice of words was so surprising I suspected that what he said was true for him, truer than the instructions from his agent! I tried not to quiver at his practiced skill which was an attempt to restore the emotional atmosphere and get me off the subject of our future family. I demanded coldly, "Is that your real reason? You want to go on forever as we are? And only as we are?"

His hand leaped off my body and his face became hot and red. I thought he would be furiously angry and I tightened my muscles to spring out of bed, away from him, but he surprised me by the sudden blurted admission, "I don't want to share a woman. That is what I have always feared. To share a woman's love. Children? They are the part of a woman. Closer than I can ever be. And I hate the thought. I will not share my women."

I reached for my robe and moved out of bed while he watched my every motion. He appeared half-angry, half-frightened now, uneasy over my own response. I was so disillusioned by this childish confession of his that

150

I wanted to hurt him, to rouse and make a man of him, but I only succeeded in rousing his adolescent craving for my body again with all of an adolescent's interest in pure sensation.

". . . He is like an irresponsible young stallion," I thought. ". . . Not adult at all."

When he reached across the bed for me, I eluded his groping fingers, saw them clench into a fist and I said abruptly, "You've got to hurry. You'll be expected back at the studio, and you musn't keep them waiting."

Karl's balled fist struck the bed hard, but the blow was impotent, only jarring the mattress, muffling the sound of his explosive temper. I looked back as I was going into my dressing room, and though I gazed at my husband, the most awful depression washed over me as I realized: "We will never be more than lovers. He never wanted me in any other way, and it is my fault. I married him without love."

It was like getting drunk to blot out unhappiness, only to find the hangover doubled the misery.

"You need not think, because you turn from me, that all women do!" Karl blurted out then. "I could have anyone. Any woman in Hollywood!"

"I'm sure you could . . . and have had," I said quietly, suddenly sorry for him as I left the room.

It was a few days later that the Clinic for Nervous Diseases which Father had endowed called me from its Valley offices and asked me to fill in for another movie star's wife who was with her husband in Iran on location. The job was mostly secretarial, and a busy one. I took it quickly enough because I found our Beverly Hills hotel life about as unsatisfactory as a nomad gypsy camp. I didn't object to Karl's fans who collected outside the studio walls to yell at him as he drove in and out, but I did hate to step out of the elevator into the private hall leading to our hotel suite and be startled by a girl, leaping out of the darkness to beg me for a pair of Karl's used socks, or even a handkerchief. And worse.

I remember one unforgettable evening, for many reasons. It was the night before the Academy Awards. There was one of those girls waylaying me just inside our foyer.

"Oh, Mrs. Dorn, is he really as sexy and marvelous in real life as he was in 'The Strange Lovers'?"

"I can't say. I never saw 'The Strange Lovers.'" I was tired and unnerved after a long tieup on the Freeway in the unfamiliar Jaguar I had given Karl for his birthday and borrowed back. Now this stringy-haired, sloppily dressed girl had given me a terrific start, jumping out at me when I thought myself alone as I unlocked the foyer door.

"He was marvy in 'Mad Winter.' He hit the girl, but it was love. Didn't you think so?"

I pushed the hall door open again, wondering what hotel employee she had bribed and for how little.

"You'll have to go now. My husband can't possibly see you here. He will be shooting until very late."

I switched on the foyer lamp. The girl really was harmless. In her shiny eyes I could read the imaginary romance she had created between herself and my husband. I had done the same at her age, and with more harm to myself; for I had idiolized Jacques Levescu! Nevertheless, I would like to have nipped in the bud the girl's crush.

"Promise you will tell him Clarice's Gang is really hummy for him."

Whatever *hummy* was. I said "I promise. Goodbye."

She was still talking when I closed and locked the hall door. We had hired a temporary cook, but it was her day off and the hotel maid we had borrowed was in her own room with the television on very loud. Everything about this place, this nomad way of life, the tight little city itself, was foreign to me, even the climate. I got into a warm tub, and spent a restful half hour among moun-

152

tainous waves of milky bubbles, hoping Karl wouldn't want to go out on the town tonight again. His agent had said it was important for him to be seen around the right places as much as possible before the Awards.

"How can I be so selfish?" I asked myself. Nobody knew better than I how very much these Awards, this Oscar in particular, meant to Karl's whole career. And yet, I lay there luxuriating in a sunken Roman Bath that they called a tub, and I kept wondering where Luc was at this moment, and if he ever thought of me. Were there other women who shared the magic, the fireworks of love with him in deserted deck chairs at midnight? The last time I had read about him, he had wrecked his Cortot Cormorant on the sand dunes of Holland but, according to the newspapers, was unhurt. For that, at least, I thanked God. There had been no mention of Claire, and I wondered. But, of course, it was no business of mine.

Luc, I murmured to myself . . . Luc, my darling. . . .

Even the name, spoken barely above a whisper, aroused me, gave me that dazzling half-pain, half delight in the pit of my body that no other man had aroused.

The telephone chimed and after a minute or two I heard the maid Rubie's voice replying. It was a brief conversation. She seemed excited and hurried along through my dressing room, calling me.

"Mrs. Dorn . . . it's long distance. . . . Important! Mrs. Dorn!"

I had already wrapped my dripping body in a big terry cloth robe and was hurrying to the bedroom telephone extension. For a second or two I couldn't identify the man's agitated voice:

"Kay! Is that you? Kay, there has been trouble. Myra is . . . ill."

"What do you mean—ill? Who is this?" Then I realized it was Mike's voice, but changed and queerly emotional.

153

Not like him with his calm competence. "Where are you, Mike?"

"San Francisco. University Hospital. You see Myra—well, we quarrelled, and Myra flew here and when I came after her, she took some pills. It's ghastly. I love her. . . . You know that, Kay! I really love her."

Mother had found out about Chiye Mitsushima's son! I began to be frantic. It occurred to me quite suddenly that I cared for Mother and that, in other circumstances, she might have been the woman Aunt Grace was.

"Yes, yes. Never mind that. Is she— How is she now? I'll get the first plane up. Or charter one. . . . Is Aunty there, at the Hospital?"

"Myra is still in coma. They say there's a chance of pneumonia. They say—"

"I'll be there tonight. Look for me. Have a car at the airport. See if Aunty can get me a police escort. How is Aunty taking it?"

"You know her. Strong as a horse when she started giving orders. She's a bit tuckered out now. But she'll come around."

"Look after Aunty. She isn't as young as she might seem to be. Goodbye."

Not that anything would happen to Aunt Grace. She was one of the Immortals. But Mother was the sort to whom things were bound to happen. And now, a suicide attempt. *Oh, Mother! You are such a fool, but you are my mother. . . .*

I began stripping off my robe on the way to my dressing room, calling out orders to the nervous Rubie. By the time I was dressed, she had a small bag packed, along with my much-used, fitted canvas makeup case into which I hastily tossed some items of makeup that Mother could wear. Nothing, I knew, would speed her recovery like a lip liner, mascara, the right blushers and a foundation to restore her natural color. Rubie had ordered a cab and

154

gotten me a seat on the third San Francisco airliner she tried for. I failed to get Karl at the studio and scribbled a note to him, explaining that he could reach me at either the hospital or Aunt Grace's old house in Pacific Heights.

The cab ride clear out to International Airport seemed to take forever and then the plane was held up on takeoff, maddeningly because the trays of dinner hadn't been loaded on board! I bit all my nails to the quick and then remembered Mother's beautiful, well-kept hands. Who would have thought she would take Mike's "past" so seriously? And yet, I had been afraid of this, all along.

By the time I reached the hospital in San Francisco, it was nearly nine o'clock that evening. Aunt Grace was sitting in a wheel chair near the Receptionist's Desk. I rushed up to her.

"Aunty! Are you—?"

"Perfectly all right. Never better," she said briskly, though she looked tired, as well she might. "It's just my sneaky way of resting while I wait. That silly woman took those pills in my house. Gave me quite a scare."

"I can imagine! I'm so sorry. But it was a shock. I suppose she had learned about Mike's previous—family."

"Hmph," said Aunt Grace. "That woman acts as if she was the only woman who'd ever been deceived." She looked at me and smiled. "Poor devil! I confess, I do know how she felt, though no man's worth a mouthful of sleeping pills."

"How is she?"

"Depends on any complications." Aunty's lovely face looked a little pinched. There were razor-fine lines around her mouth. I hadn't seen her since my marriage, and my heart twisted painfully at the signs of age I began to notice in her. Would I chance losing her too one day soon?

Even Aunt Grace admitted, when our first night of

155

waiting was over, that Mike showed up as a better man than she had thought. Aunt Grace took her own room in the Hospital and used it to get a little sleep the next day, as I did, but Mike remained on the alert until ten that morning when Mother was able to see him for a few minutes. Neither Aunt Grace nor I was permitted to speak with her yet, but Mike was not reticent in discussing the causes of Mother's suicide attempt. As I had supposed, Mother found out about Chiye's son. Mike explained to us over breakfast in the hospital restaurant downstairs.

"Myra insisted on hiring Chiye away from you, Kay. Offered her more money, better conditions. Or so she said. At any rate, Chiye showed up with my boy, and the minute Myra caught a look at the little tyke, she knew. She and Chiye had words, and when I interfered, Myra went wild. Said I'd chosen Chiye. She left me. The next thing I knew, your Aunt Grace was calling me from here. Myra must have taken every Seconal she had. I've always fought against her getting those prescriptions filled. But you know Myra. Nobody can argue with her." His big frame shuddered. He rubbed his face tiredly. "All the same, there's nobody like her. For me. She needs me, you know. Always has. Needs somebody to treat her like a little girl. Spoil her."

A nurse stuck her neat head in Aunt Grace's room, interrupting Mike's spirited defense of Mother.

"A call for Mrs. Dorn. Shall we have it switched here to Miss Amberley's room?"

"It must be my husband." I took up the phone.

"Kay darling, how is your mother?"

"Still holding her own. We can't be sure yet."

There was an awkward pause. He scarcely knew Mother. He had no reason to share any of my own mixed emotions, but even before he spoke again, I had a feeling his slightly breathless excitement concernd somthing quite different.

156

"Kay darling. . . . It is of first importance—I must know about tonight."

"Tonight?"

"The Awards. The Oscars. There will be the cameras upon the Nominees, you understand. What am I to do?"

"Oh, Karl, take someone from the studio. Don't you see? We won't even know about Mother for hours yet. But I wish you all the luck in the world."

He laughed in the embarrassed way I remembered with affection. I wished I could care more about his Award.

"*Variety*'s poll says I will win. But these things . . . One is never sure." He hesitated. "If you can not return by this evening—"

"I'm afraid not, darling."

". . . then the studio suggests Lisa Kestner."

"Wonderful. She is very photogenic."

And that was that. I found I couldn't even be jealous. But I felt that Karl deserved the Award for many of his acting roles, and during the day when I thought of him at all, I kept hoping he would win.

Mother was put under oxygen late in the afternoon. Complications had set in. I couldn't understand my feelings, my anxiety. Perhaps it was because she was the only parent I had. Or even the purely selfish identification I made with Mother. I seemed to have messed my own life almost as much as Mother had ruined hers. During these awful hours when time dragged and I was witness to Mike's self-recriminations, his useless regrets for what might have been, I thought very seriously of my own shortcomings and the failure of my own life in marriage.

While Mike and I were waiting in the Green Room Lounge nearest Mother's room that night, Aunt Grace sent for me. She had been watching television, the Academy Awards.

157

"Look!" she said, pointing to the high screen of the TV set.

There was a confusion of applause, many faces vaguely familiar to me from old movies. And then, in the center stage, making his bow, Karl Dorn, looking slight and frightened and endearing.

"He won!" I yelled.

"Good lad," said Aunt Grace slowly, without her usual force. "Probably too good for you, Katy my dear. I wish you'd start that family of yours soon. I like the looks of that boy."

I agreed but I was too busy watching the television activity at the big Santa Monica Auditorium to wonder at Aunt Grace's unexpectedly meek voice. Karl was radiant as he stammered, "My thanks to America for her generosity to a stranger, and to my wife, and my many friends in the Industry—to all of you." He embraced them all with his widespread arms and the cameras closed on his ingratiating grin. I was warmed and happy for him.

I became aware of a sound between a sigh and a gasp behind me and looked back at Aunt Grace's bed. She had closed her eyes in pain. Her face looked pinched and shadowed, frightening. I rang the bell to summon a nurse. The shaking of my fingers surprised me. I couldn't ever remember being so panicked. Aunt Grace would hate it if I behaved badly now. Trying not to alarm her, I asked in the calmest tones I could manage, "Where does it hurt, Aunty?"

Between pale lips she muttered, "Something I ate . . . no doubt," but her body stiffened and writhed and I thought prayerfully, "Don't let me lose her."

Aunty whispered, "No—fuss—girl."

A nurse came bustling in, all cheer and easy chiding. "Now, now, mustn't upset the hospital routine for our little errands; must we?"

158

Aunt Grace became her old salty self momentarily. "Hmph. Just wanted you to—change the channel on that—Idiot Box."

The nurse's first reaction was amused impatience, but as I motioned to her and she glanced at Aunty's huddled figure on the bed, she became quietly efficient.

"Is she all right?" I asked a couple of times, stupidly, because the nurse was so busy. As soon as the doctor arrived, I was sent out of the room in the charge of Mike who had come to tell me the reports on Mother were better. Tense and cold, with hardly a word to say to each other, Mike and I, and later Hildy, looking very old, sat up our second night's vigil. I knew even before the doctors came to explain, that Aunt Grace's indigestion was actually the beginnings of a heart attack, but through the night it was impressive to see how many people came hurrying to be there in the hospital, to join our vigil, not for poor Mother, but for Aunt Grace.

"We are all deeply sorry here at the hospital," Dr. Steinberg told us at one time, looking as though he had been under great strain. "Everything is being tried. Believe me." He began to enumerate the great heart machinery set in motion, but I scarcely understood his technical terms. I was praying as I hadn't prayed since I was a child. I would not have admitted it to anyone, especially Mike, but if I had to make a trade, I knew in my heart that Myra Amberley was not worth the life of Aunt Grace.

People kept coming to speak to me, whispering that Aunt Grace hadn't looked well lately, that she worked too hard . . . things I knew and blamed myself for. And Mother's suicide attempt had given Aunty's poor, sturdy old heart one last jolt.

Along toward morning the Green Room in which we were waiting became very silent. The other visitors left.

159

But all during these hours I was told, the Hospital switchboard was swamped with calls about Aunty.

One of Mother's doctors came to us at seven-thirty in the morning to tell us that Mother was out of danger. While Mike was rejoicing, I watched the doctor. His grave face told me the rest of the story.

Aunt Grace had died minutes before.

THIRTEEN/

THERE ARE LOSSES too great for tears. I found myself enormously grateful for the crowded hours of work following Aunty's death. There were the threads of all the businesses, corporations, endowments, charities and, of course, the immediate necessity, before the funeral, of meeting and presenting an intelligent, unemotional face to the many distinguished friends of hers who arrived for the services.

As well as I had known her, I was surprised at the names of the funeral guests as I went over them in Aunty's warm, red victorian parlor: A U.S. Senator, the governor, a Supreme Court Justice, representatives of nine foreign countries, including one name I should not have been surprised to see, that of Her Serene Highness, Princess Sophie-Frederick of Feldenstein.

It had been impossible to keep the news of Aunty's death from Mother, but in her case, my concern was merely that the announcement of one person's death to another who had faced death so recently, would send Mother into a depression and slow her recovery. I knew that Mother had never borne Aunt Grace much love, and the feeling or lack of it, was reciprocated. Nevertheless, Mother began to be very anxious to be on her feet, and though it was impossible for her to attend the funeral, she hinted strongly that she would like to meet some of Aunty's mourners. Then I understood her concern.

"The Princess will be here. She's the one you want to meet; isn't she, Mother?"

"Well, sweetie, Grace always promised to arrange an introduction to Sophie-Frederick. Naturally, I've met the handsome heir, Prince Stefan, but—a reigning monarch! Well, you must admit that makes her special."

"She was Aunt Grace's friend. That makes her special."

Mother smiled. "I stand corrected. But do bring her to see me. Now, will you call Mike in?"

"Are you going back to him, Mother?"

She considered her carefully made up face in the hand mirror before dropping it on her bedcovers.

"My dear Kay, I never intended to leave him. I wanted to teach him a lesson; that's all."

"You nearly taught yourself a lesson—a fatal lesson," I reminded her, but it was wasted breath, and I left soon after. It depressed me terribly to be in the hospital, to pass the door of the room that had been Aunt Grace's, and to remember that when I returned to the old house in Pacific Heights, she wouldn't be there with her gruff, bold manner, her courage, her wonderful ability to handle any situation, any emergency or problem. Sometimes, I cried at night, in bed, but I hated to have anyone know.

Karl flew up to spend a few hours with me on the day before the funeral. At first, I believed I might find great comfort in his presence as well as his full and detailed description of the Academy Award aftermath, with photographers blinding him, and the rest of the night blanked out by champagne plus his hysterical happiness over the Oscar. I still felt guilty that I could not have

162

been with him in that moment so precious to him, and I tried to concentrate on enjoying every word of his dramatized version of the event.

But Karl had to return that evening for important scenes which he claimed could only be shot on the day of the funeral. The next morning proved to be so busy, I hardly missed him at all. I was at Aunt Grace's desk in the Victorian Parlor, trying to understand the complex structure of Amberley World Centers, Limited, when Hildy came in, trying with amusing effort, to cross the worn carpet on tiptoe.

"Glory Be! She's a-waiting in the hall. In this very house. Just like anybody."

I looked up, a little vague, wrapped up as I was in the tentacles of international corporate structure with which I hoped to blot out thoughts of the funeral later in the day.

"Is it Mother?"

"Katy, I never thought I'd see the day. That Majesty person. Her High and Mightiness."

I got up quickly. I had expected the Princess to stand on her dignity and summon me to her hotel suite. It was an impressive, and, to me, beautiful proof of her affection for Aunt Grace that she had come here to Aunty's old home, with none of the ceremony which very small nations so often demanded as their right. I said to Hildy, "Don't let her wait in that drafty hall, for Heaven's sake. Ask her— Never mind. I'll go."

I don't quite know how I expected the Princess to differ from the pictures of her that I had seen in newspapers such as the regal portrait widely published at the time of the Twentieth Anniversary of her accession to power. That was nearly four years ago and Aunt Grace had flown to Feldenstein to be present as Her Highness' guest in the Palace itself. They had urged me to visit the little country too, but I knew their object was to promote a

163

romance between me and Prince Stefan Nicolaievich, and was too contrary to oblige the matchmakers. From all I had heard, the Prince shared my dislike of having his life maneuvered.

"Is she alone?" I whispered.

"A long-nosed, simpering female is with her. Lady-in-Waiting, or something. And then, there's the man."

"Her son?" It seemed strange that they would both be gone from their little principality at the same time.

As I stepped into the hall and saw the three people waiting, I thought no Hollywood actress could do justice to the tall, regal woman with her white hair piled high and adding to her natural height and dignity. The lady-in-waiting simpered, as Hildy said, and looked amusingly agitated as she tried to introduce us. Almost without planning the gesture, I bent one knee in a slight curtsey and the Princess took my hands and drew me to her. She touched her lips to my forehead and then stood off, still holding my hands and looking me up and down. Her voice, as she spoke, was faintly accented. French, I thought.

"My dear! What can I say of our loss? My dearest friend, she was."

I managed to express my pleasure at her coming, but I was still very much in awe of her, and almost forgot to ask her if she had found her hotel suite satisfactory. She surprised me again by saying she had sent her bags to the St. Francis Hotel where she had stayed on previous visits, and had come directly to Grace Amberley's home. While I was marvelling and giving orders for her immediate use of one of the suites upstairs, she laughed lightly.

"Thank you, but do not suppose I come direct to you from pure affection, my dear. It is that there were journalists waiting at the hotel to snap their so-candid pictures of me." She turned to the woman who accompanied her

164

and began to remove her gloves with gestures that seemed graceful, yet imperious, to the very bone. The hall was so dark, I did not make out the features of the man behind her and her lady-in-waiting until she moved toward the stairs. I prepared, with some curiosity, to meet Prince Stefan Nicolaievich, but instead, I was shaken by the unexpected sight of Luc Sebastiani. He took my hand, said quietly, with the intent look I remembered so well, "You are looking pale, but lovelier than ever, Kay."

I thanked him shakily, grateful too that he had not at once mentioned my loss. I was still confused when the Princess looked down at us from the stair landing.

"Luc was anxious to attend the funeral. He was an old friend of Grace's."

"Yes, I remember." I remembered with a rueful smile, that he and Claire had known Aunt Grace before they knew me. I said aloud, with a small laugh, "Luc and Claire gave Aunty the full itinerary of my first honeymoon."

"Cheer her up, my dear Luc. I will join you shortly. Come along, Babette."

The elderly woman named Babette had very much dyed, high-piled red hair, which was in frivolous conflict with her long, wolfhound's face.

"Claire wasn't able to come?" I asked as Luc and I went into the Parlor. It was a remark more polite than sincere. I couldn't forget Claire's eagerness to hurt Mother through me. She had carefully witnessed Mother's wedding to Mike and only afterward, with just as great care, sent me to discover the truth about Mike's past. It seemed to me a deliberately malevolent trick.

"No," Luc said, borrowing my own casual tone. "I am afraid not. She has been ill." As I looked up, guilty over my own suspicions, he added, "It is a chronic illness. These attacks have come several times before."

165

I said I was very sorry, and we began to talk of the Princess and her remarkable hand at ruling.

"She manages to balance her influence with all her neighbors," Luc explained. "A very shrewd woman. I admire her more than I can say. Even when the great powers are quarreling, Her Serene Highness is the arbiter. But Miss Amberley was a frequent visitor. It is odd we never met you there." I was pouring Scotch for him from Aunt Grace's old crystal decanter and at that betraying "we" I asked as cuttingly as I could, "By 'we', you mean yourself and Claire, of course."

"Sometimes. Not always." He had been about to drink but he looked at me now over the glass and said simply, "Kay, I should have told you. Long ago." But then he took a long, bitter drink and did not go on.

The mere way he pronounced my name affected me as his quiet voice, his direct, yet veiled gaze had affected me long ago, almost from the moment of our meeting. Something about him, even then, had suggested a brooding unhappiness, something bitter that he carried with him. That was years ago and whatever secret troubled him then had not left him during all the years since. Claire was in it somehow. Or at least her absence was a part of his unhappiness. This thought sickened me and I was grateful when Princess Frederick came into the room and asked Hildy most politely if she and Lady Babette Wallenburg might have champagne.

"Sure, Highness," Hildy agreed, in her flat way. "If you'll go for the local brand."

We all laughed except Lady Babette who appeared shocked, then, borrowing her mood from her mistress, she looked on the cheerful side. "For Madame," she said with her not-unlikeable little smirk, "one might call your California champagne the imported variety."

"Very true, Babette," the Princess flattered her. "You are witty today."

166

I became aware, as before in Luc's presence, of the tie between us, the feeling of unity and even warmth as we looked at each other, sharing an unobtrusive amusement over Lady Babette's flutters of pleasure when complimented by her mistress. I realized that it required no effect at conversation, no attempts to fill in the silence between Luc and me. And then the Princess said abruptly as Hildy filled her champagne glass, "Do we meet your husband this afternoon, Kay? I have seen his films. He is a charming young man."

Exceedingly aware of Luc who had looked suddenly and attentively into his own glass, I said without expression, "I'm afraid he can't be here for the funeral. They are shooting some important scenes today." I was almost sure Lady Babette's admiring glance at the Princess said: "How right you were!" and the notion of the Princess predicting the failure of my marriage was enough to put me on my mettle. Whether I had made another marital mistake or not, I wasn't going to have a stranger tell me so.

"Karl has been with me almost constantly since Aunty became ill. But of course, this absence was unavoidable."

I may have been mistaken but I thought my enthusiastic mention of Karl disappointed her. What persistent creatures matchmakers were! Nevertheless, I was slightly unnerved by the presence of Luc, his firm, lean body so near mine, the sensitivity to his nearness. I told myself I only imagined a similar sensitivity in him because I wanted it to be there. But it was impossible to ignore the effect of Luc's presence, and I was almost grateful when Hildy came stalking in to announce that several reporters were hounding her for pictures of us and interviews with the Princess. As though Aunty's funeral were a kind of gathering place for international celebrities!

"Also," Hildy added to me in the loudest whisper of

167

which she was capable, "they're asking if you being here and Mr. Dorn being in L.A. at a time like this means you've gone *phfft*."

Everyone but Luc looked at me. Luc went to the window and gazed out. "They seem to be getting into the house."

I was in the midst of giving Hildy an angry denial to deliver to them when the first of the reporters looked into the parlor. He appeared harmless enough, a small, reedy fellow in slacks, sweater and jacket, who looked as though he'd just popped off a western college campus.

"Sorry, M'am. That is— Ladies . . . Sir. The door was open. I figured you'd rather talk here than at the cemetery. Quite a crowd expected. Shows how popular Miss Amberley was. Everybody was crazy about her, you know."

"I had better be on my way," said the Princess. "Luc, why do you not handle these tiresome creatures for Kay? Babette, come along. What time is the service, my dear?"

I told her, and then added hurriedly, not wanting to spend the next difficult hour in Luc's company, "I really should see the reporters myself."

Luc turned back from the window. "If you wish, but I would like to speak to you, if I may. Perhaps when the press people are gone."

In a panic that baffled me by its grip on me, I laughed and motioned him toward the Princess.

"Please don't be offended, Luc, but we can talk later. I might as well settle this newspaper interview thing now."

The young reporter had stepped aside and tried to say something to the Princess as she passed him, going into the hall. I was fascinated at her masterly way of avoiding him. She raised her eyebrows, looked through him, smiling coolly into space, and managed to pass the gauntlet of three other reporters, male and female, without being touched or spoken to. Lady Babette had less luck, or more likely her technique was not so skillful, but as Hildy went after the ladies to try and get the press better organized, Luc said to me in a low voice, "Pardon, Kay. Her Highness is familiar with our life, mine and Claire's, and she believes I should tell you why our behavior at times must have seemed strange to you."

Seeing the young reporter had pricked up his ears, I said hurriedly, "Another time. I've got to be at Cadeau's Chapel in less than an hour."

In spite of my deep attraction to him, I hoped he did not intend to make excuses in which he began with the hackneyed "Claire doesn't understand me." On the other hand I wanted even less to have him apologize for the few moments I had experienced with him in the deck chair on shipboard, and later, under the Hau tree at *Makai*.

Luc followed my glance at the reporter and agreed without saying anything. As he left and I sat down to answer the reporter's questions, he looked back at me once, briefly, with that direct, unsmiling gaze that always moved me deeply. What had he been about to say? What excuses, and for what particular action? I did not want excuses. I only wanted him to remember our moments together as I remembered them.

As I tried to lead the several reporters' questions onto the subject of Aunt Grace's long, productive life, suggesting they see my secretary downtown for certain business facts, I wondered what secret in Luc's and Claire's marriage could possibly be of interest to Princess Sophie-Frederick.

Karl telephoned me as I was getting rid of the reporters including the boy who had heard Luc's conversation with me. I was pleased that Karl had been thoughtful enough to call today of all days, when I needed the assurance that he still cared a little for me, in spite of the note of indifference upon which we had parted.

"My darling," he said with great feeling, "I am very guilty, not to be with you on this terrible day for you. But we are so busy. So much to do. And then, everywhere I am beseiged for interviews. Because of the Oscar, you understand."

"Of course I understand, Karl. Don't work too hard. Maybe I can be back there in a couple of days."

There was a distinct and noticeable silence.

"Are you still there?" I asked uneasily, beginning to wonder.

"Hello? Hello?" Karl repeated several times. "Darling, I believe we have been cut off. I cannot hear you."

Only slightly reassured I repeated that I might be able to get away in two days. Karl was warmly enthusiastic, with reservations. "Try then, my darling. Try to make it by the weekend, but you must not rush away from your duty only to please me. I will not expect you until the weekend."

"Fine. That should give me four or five days. Take care of yourself."

"And you, my darling."

We cut off the connection. It had not been the most promising conversation for the future of our marriage, but maybe if I tried harder, delegated Aunty's many responsibilities to men and women who knew them better than I did, I could devote all my time to being purely a wife to Karl.

The funeral service was not as painful as it might have been. Princess Frederick had some wonderful anecdotes about her girlhood days with Aunty, and following her lead, others too remembered Aunty with humor and gusto, as Aunt Grace herself would have wished to be remembered. It was Luc who quietly and unobtrusively took the place beside me which would normally have been Karl's place. Hildy and I had assured each other we would not cry during the Chapel Service. We knew how Aunt Grace hated tears. But the sight of Hildy's dear, well-scrubbed and stoic face at the graveside as it broke up into unshed tears affected me horribly, and it was Luc who asked me at that minute, "Miss Amberley's father chose this burial ground? It is a place of great beauty."

"Her grand-uncle chose it, actually." I tried to laugh. "He was always very provident. He planned ahead."

"An excellent virtue," he agreed and took my hand comfortingly. We both looked down, first at our fingers interlaced, then at the soft, spongy grass underfoot. Slowly, guiltily, we freed our hands and stepped apart. At the same time a photographer on the gravel road below the graves set off a big flash, aiming his camera at the two of us. I knew that one more moment had been preserved for posterity for no other reason than that many shrewd ancestors had made me, by pure chance, the richest girl in the world. I would never do anything in my life worthwhile; or merely personal and sad as this, that would overshadow the title I had inherited through no fault or skill of my own.

The Princess and Lady Babette rode back to town with Luc and me and it was agreed that the four of us, with Aunty's other old friend, the Senator, would have a quiet dinner in the Princess' hotel suite. I did not want to be alone with Luc, not only because of Karl, but because it would be despicable, I felt, to tempt fate in this way behind Claire's back. During the day I had begun to wonder, though nothing was said on the subject, whether the problem with the Sebastianis was not Claire's health, but her rejection of Luc. Just being together, however, told Luc and me a great deal about our feelings for each other. Not a word or suggestion of intimacy took place between us beyond that comforting gesture on Luc's part at the grave, but he shared my deep awareness of the emotional ties between us.

171

It was just before Luc and the Senator left for their own hotels that the Princess asked me to remain for a late-evening cordial and a few minutes of talk about my future plans.

Lady Babette poured gold-flecked drops of Goldwasser, an almost forgotten liqueur I had not tasted in many years, and as the Princess' shrewd eyes stared into the golden depths of the glass, she said calmly, "Luc Sebastiani will never be able to obtain a divorce."

A little flushed, I managed to remark, "Their religion, no doubt. But, of course, their married life is not really my business."

"No, my dear, not their religion. I remember the wedding, nearly a score of years ago. He was very much in love. A mechanic who showed great aptitude for the motors of Cortot. In those days Claire modelled for one of those small, post-war couturiers in Florence. She was my own vendeuse and I took a fancy to her romance with Sebastiani, that wild, brooding Corsican. Claire is a gorgeous creature, you know. One always notices that first."

I agreed.

"Well, then. But I have never felt that Claire's feeling —of that sort—was as deep, though theirs was a reasonably happy marriage. However, Luc wanted children very much, and Claire wanted them not at all. About ten years or so ago, Claire had what was called . . . an accident, while she was *enciente*. You take my meaning?"

"Perfectly." Yet it was such an old-fashioned word for a woman as modern and direct as the Princess.

"At any rate, there was a miscarriage, and Claire developed curious habits. She tried to arrange intimacies between Luc and other women. I doubt if Luc permitted himself to be used in this way, but I happen to know she maneuvered him into an appearance, at least, of intimacy with my Mistress of the Wardrobe, and then tried to blackmail the woman. Foolishly, Natalie paid her. From

172

what Luc has intimated, Claire tried this between you and Luc. It is Claire's attempt to earn what she once told me was the fortune she felt she deserved."

Puzzled, for Luc had confessed to this on shipboard, I asked, "Is she quite sane?"

The Princess drank down the cordial, gold flecks and all.

"That is the crux of the problem. She has her lucid moments. She seems normal for months at a time. Then come the months when she . . . vegetates. No one can communicate with her. She simply turns off all relationships with the world. During those periods she receives excellent care at a private clinic in which I am interested."

"And she always recovers?" I asked, torn between shock and pity. Pity for both of them.

"Invariably. She seems herself, but she is not strong, of course. She rests a good deal. She is delicate. A matter of the blood, you know."

"He must love her very much to remain so faithful."

"Quite." The Princess looked at me in her penetrating way, as though she read my soul. "It is not the kind of love it once was. Not, I think, the kind he is capable of offering a mature woman. But a parental love, perhaps. He feels responsible, you see. The pity is, there will never be the normal family life he once dreamed of. There is no question of Claire's ever having children."

"What a tragedy for both of them!" The story explained so much about the behavior of Luc and Claire, her brittle, glassy lightness of manner, and the bitterness, the sombre quality I had always felt in Luc.

"Now, my dear, since we have dispensed with unpleasant subjects," the Princess said briskly, handing her glass to Lady Babette for a refill. "When are you coming to visit Stefan Nicolaievich and me?"

"Not for some time, I'm afraid. And naturally, a great

173

deal depends upon my husband's work. I am married, don't forget." I said this lightly, not wishing to offend her, but I felt that she was pressing too hard and behaving in too proprietary a manner toward a woman she had barely met. Nothing could shake her confidence, apparently.

"You are married *now*, to be sure. But if, in future. . . ."

"I'll ask Karl when it would be convenient for him to make the trip with me," I promised.

We smiled at each other with the utmost in good manners.

FOURTEEN/

In spite of my boast, Karl did not visit Feldenstein with me, even when, the following year, the Princess kindly issued personal invitations to attend the Silver Jubilee Anniversary of her accession to power. Meanwhile, after Aunty's funeral, I knew almost the moment I returned to Beverly Hills that Karl had not been alone in the suite during my absence. I said nothing, pretending not to notice the telltale signs: the stray cigarettes tucked away in my dressing table, though Karl despised cigarettes and invariably smoked his precious pipe; the loose, wispy feathers on the floor of my dressing room, though I would rather die than be caught wearing feathers. And most significant of all, when we made love, he was extremely knowing about the stimulus of erogenous zones on and in the human body. I was far from objecting to him as a lover, but our lives beyond the frame of a kingsize bed, seemed more and more divergent.

I remained in Southern California almost continuously, so long as Karl's filming kept him there, but his particular forte was proving to be the brutally sensuous, civilized-savage, and such films were logically based in more exotic locales, which meant constant location trips to the Near and Far East, and occasionally the Mediterranean. I went with him when he wished it, but it was evident to both of us that except for a limited area, we had almost nothing in common, and during much of his location shooting, I spent the time reorganizing and getting to understand Aunt Grace's work in the Amberley Empire.

When we received the invitation to attend Feldenstein's Silver Jubilee which was to take place in five months, Karl reminded me that he would be in the midst of filming in Japan during that particular month, and I wrote, both to the Princess and her Chancellor, explaining the necessity for our refusal of the honor. It was on the night Karl was packing for the flight to Japan that things were ended between us.

He said suddenly, "My darling, you do not really want to make the trip; do you?"

I was so surprised I almost dropped the transistor which he was taking rather as one carries coals to Newcastle. Hildy stopped in the midst of packing my last bag to ask abruptly, "What's all this? Ain't you going?"

I had asked Hildy where she preferred to be, and she chose to divide her time between San Francisco and Beverly Hills. I was not surprised that her presence now annoyed my husband, but she had always been a part of my life and I could not imagine being without her for long.

Karl scowled at her but she did nothing until I said carefully, "Hildy, would you mind seeing how Rubie is getting along with Karl's fan mail?"

"Sure. All you gotta do is ask," and away she klomped.

I looked at my husband, knowing this was the crisis, and feeling numb, but my hands were cold. "I want to make the trip because it's your job. Why wouldn't I?" I tried to make him look at me, but he was shy about it. Not at all his usual bold self.

"Because . . . I thought you might have wished to attend to your affairs—"

"Affairs!"

He was startled. "No, no. I meant . . . You neglect your own life for me. Your social life, the life of your so-rich Amberley affairs. It is unfair of me to take you from them so often."

"Thank you. That is thoughtful of you." And unusual, I added to myself, wondering what he really had in mind. I tried to understand my own emotions, but I still seemed numb, a little confused. "Then, you think I shouldn't make the trip at all?"

He began to finger his cufflinks, twisting them until it made me so nervous I had to look away.

"That is to say—you see— There have been times when we were apart and, naturally, I felt the desire for a woman."

"Naturally."

He stared at me. "You knew?"

"Darling," I said, "you are only human. I think that's the term."

He seemed ashamed of my knowledge, or perhaps the confession that followed. "*Ja*. It is so. But now, I am afraid I have been careless. And the scandal you can imagine!"

This time I sat down abruptly on the bed. I felt sick, far sicker than I could imagine feeling over what my brain told me had been an inevitable parting.

"How do you mean—'careless'?"

"You know." He leaned over the bed, reaching for my hand. I let my fingers rest in his, without really feeling his pressure. "My poor darling, how can I tell you? It was so stupid! Incredibly stupid!"

177

"In other words, you've gotten some girl pregnant and she threatens to make a scandal that will hurt your career."

He smiled sheepishly. "Well, not precisely a girl. But the rest is unfortunately true."

"Who is she?"

I wondered at his hesitation, then understood when he said, "As a matter of fact, you know her. It is Lisa Kestner."

After the horrible, bubbly little silence that followed, I saw the humor of it and began to laugh. I couldn't seem to stop for a minute or two. He became more nervous than ever and I think he would have followed the established cinema practice of shaking me if I hadn't pulled away.

"If you thought about it, Karl, you'd see the poetic justice of it. I took you away from her in the first place. And I wanted children. She's got you back, but you have to take the children with her."

It was not a very elegant or adult parting. He failed to see the humor of the situation. It was the last time we met before the involved red tape of the divorce, during which my lawyers claimed Karl's lawyers were holding them up over community property. I told them to forget the quarrel and settle as soon as possible. I didn't care very much what happened to Lisa Kestner, but I did have some feeling for the baby whose legitimacy might be of some importance to him or her one day. Karl and Lisa were understandably anxious to get a Mexican divorce, and since I now wanted to get back to my own life, enormously complicated as a result of my long intermittent absences, I gave them whatever legal help was needed.

I was in the Islands at *Makai* when Mother and Mike flew over, as Mother put it, "to comfort me in my loneliness." Mother thoughtfully brought me the *Los Angeles Times* where there was a chummy picture on the second

178

page, showing "famed new idol and Oscar winner Karl Dorn" and Lisa taking their vows in Tijuana. It all had a dreadfully reminiscent ring. I thought, with increasing bitterness and self-contempt, of that first marriage of mine. And now, here was Lisa Kestner who was going to have Karl's child, the child I had wanted. She looked amazingly chic for a woman five months pregnant.

One morning, less than a week after the Kestner-Dorn wedding I was having brunch at the Outrigger Club with Ito Shimbashi, an Island friend I had known most of my life. Ann and Morgan Haight, having been directed by Mother, walked in. Ann seemed quieter than ever and Morgan more dictatorial. They were reasonably glad to see me, although Morgan's attitude toward my distinguished friend, Ito, was hardly enthusiastic. It amused Ito when I specified that Ito was one of the governor's top aides; for Morgan warmed up with ludicrous haste. Becoming conversational, Morgan suggested to Ann, "We had better show Kay the papers. They may not get all the scandal over here."

"I've seen it," I said. "If you mean Karl's marriage."

Even Ann looked a bit excited. Her pale cheeks reddened perceptibly.

"Oh, Morgan, I don't think we ought to now. Besides, Mr. Shimbashi isn't interested in people we used to know."

Ito said politely, "I am acquainted with Mr. Dorn. A charming young actor."

"For heaven's sake! Let's have it." I cut through this pussyfooting.

Ann took the folded clipping from her handbag and silently handed it across the table. I unfolded it, and held it so Ito could see it at the same time. I don't know which of us was the more surprised, but there was Lisa Kestner Dorn on the front pages of the *San Francisco Chronicle*. Her clever, attractive, middle-European face was blotched

179

up by an ugly swollen black eye. Beside this flash photo was a more fetching one of Lisa with, of all things, a white, piratical-looking eye patch over the swollen eye.

"'Just a lover's quarrel,' the fetching new Mrs. Dorn confided as she inaugurated a new fashion. According to the beautiful Lisa, the classic shiner was bestowed by her mate of seven days, German-born film star, Karl Dorn, recently divorced by Jet Setter and richest girl in the world, Kay Amberley Levescu Dorn."

Ann watched me anxiously. "What on earth do you suppose made him do such a thing? Kay! Don't tell me he ever struck you."

I was mulling over the article and especially the three-quarter shot of Lisa with the patch on her eye, and I had a good suspicion why Karl gave her that black eye. I could have sworn she wasn't pregnant, and very likely never had been during her relationship with Karl. Poor Karl! Well, when he thought it over, he would probably be delighted that he wasn't going to be a father, after all.

If I allowed myself to feel self-pity, or even more absurd, if I confessed my loneliness, I would know then just what a failure my life had been to date. To have all the money in the world, and yet to have been twice discarded by a man who married me, showed me just how useless I was. It had to be my fault that I was almost thirty, without either a man who loved and needed me, or his children, whom I needed.

I flew back home to my penthouse rather than the old home in Pacific Heights, during this period of self-examination, and gave a few parties to liven things up, mostly me. As so often happens in life, the big change, the rebirth of my self-respect, crept up on me and I hardly knew it. It was after one of those interminable parties that filled the apartment with people whose names I didn't even know, when Pegeen called me to the telephone.

"It's long distance and that exciting you wouldn't believe! A foreign-sounding gent. A real, live Count, he is. Named Stiff, or something."

I didn't really think there was anything important about Pegeen's count. He probably wanted the Amberley Foundation to establish a hospital, or some other charity in his country, whatever that might be. This sort of thing, which so many mistakenly believed was under my control, could usually be siphoned away from me by one of my secretaries or by the switchboard wherever I happened to be. Somehow, this "Stiff" person had slipped past all my protective barricade. It was hard, and often painful, to hear these incessant pleas for charity and to discover how futile was even a great fortune, to care for two and a half million begging, demanding letters a year.

As I came in from the chilly, invigorating terrace, it was shortly before two a.m. and the rooms seemed full of stale smoke and spilled liquor, drying into the carpets.

"I've got to get hold of myself and do something with my life," I thought, loathing these after-effects of a party I hadn't really wanted in the first place, whose guests, for the most part, were people I found incompatible.

The man calling me across two continents and an ocean, was introduced by a lesser functionary as Comte Gustaf von Stieff, Chancellor to Her Serene Highness, the Princess Sophie-Frederick. It was impossible not to be both flattered and touched by this gesture of the Princess' friendship.

"The matter is," he explained in very fair English, "Her Serene Highness noted in the press that Madame Dorn was now, forgive the indiscretion, of herself alone."

"Unfortunately, yes. I am of myself alone." I had a feeling I was a little high, but I also felt a sudden glow of hope, as though there were still some sparks glowing somewhere to make life again exciting and worthwhile.

"Just so. Then Her Serene Highness has graciously

181

suggested that Madame might enjoy a different kind of scene during the period of our glorious Jubilee. Madame understands that she will be the Princess Frederick's personal guest? In the Palace at Weiburg, our capital?"

I said I would think about it and that I was endlessly grateful to Her Highness for the invitation. He agreed, just a little pompously, and rang off. But before I went to bed that night, I knew I wanted to accept that once-spurned invitation. It was my fate. It came exactly when my life needed new considerations, new challenges, and undoubtedly new problems. The latter did not frighten me in the least. I welcomed them.

The Silver Jubilee had been inaugurated before I reached Weiburg, the capital of this tiny principality which was not quite as large as Luxembourg, though larger than Lichtenstein. But even before my fast express from Zurich reached the borders of Feldenstein I was aware of the importance of Princess Sophie-Frederick's name and reputation in her tiny Middle-European country. The comfortable new train was far more efficient than the criss-crossing airlines in this area where it took longer to reach Weiburg from its airport than it took to fly from Zurich or Paris to Feldenstein, and during our short time in the red plush parlor car, Pegeen and I met impressive fellow guests arriving to pay honor to the Princess. There was a delightful and witty English nobleman representing Her Britannic Majesty, a striking and equally clever feminine representative of the French Republic, and half a dozen other guests, coming from the Near-East, and from Canada and Japan, whose very character spoke highly of the world's opinion of Princess Frederick.

The city of Weiburg was neat and Eighteenth Century Hanover, an architecture that has always depressed me, but the lovely, tree-lined Frederickplatz, which most of the public buildings faced on, made up to me for the city's generally rigid look. The royal family had always straddled political fences and was as courted by the French as by its German-Austrian neighbors, so that there was no language problem for me. There was one old problem that had never changed and certainly never diminished, however. As we moved across the huge, barny, echoing station, Pegeen started to put my coat around my shoulders and then screamed. The explosion of flash bulbs, the click of miniscule cameras held up to huge, squid-like eyes, almost made me scream. It was worse than the New York and Zurich greeting.

"*Perdoneme,* Senora," said an especially persistent young journalist as he motioned his companion to raise his camera again. "Is that chinchilla?"

"No," Pegeen snapped, to my amusement. "It's Field Mouse."

Several people laughed and I hurried on, Pegeen was indignant that they had to ask such questions, as she was indignant a little later at the question fired at me from a slight distance and taken up by a number of voices: "Is it true you'll be a Princess next? . . . When is the royal engagement to be announced, Miss Amberley? . . . How does it feel to marry a Prince, Kay? Hey, Kay Amberley, turn around!"

Knowing what was proper, Peg yelled back at them, "You'll be calling her Mrs. Dorn unless you've the manners of a bog-trotter."

At that, I had to laugh, which was fortunate, as we almost collided with a striking old gentleman in a gray, full-skirted overcoat that rather resembled the German uniform of two wars. The resemblance was assisted by his white mustaches. He was accompanied by several uniformed men in the background, but more immediately by a youngish man in a similar, flattering coat, bareheaded, with dark, searching eyes that seemed luminous against his pale, olive complexion. Unruly black hair

183

helped to relieve his extraordinary good looks of the charge of effeminacy. His delightful, welcoming smile won me over at once.

The old gentleman said quickly, to his companion, "Allow me, Your Highness. I have the honor to present Madame Dorn. Madame, High Serene Highness was so anxious to meet you he had graciously consented to accompany me to greet you *in person,* as they say."

I heard Pegeen's gasp beside me and very nearly followed her example. I bobbed a brief curtsey, glad that my skirt was not tight. The Prince took both my hands, lowered his stunning head slightly and kissed me on each cheek. It was worth the long journey just for that graceful gesture. I began to think I had been a fool to avoid both the country and its bachelor prince so long. Perhaps Aunt Grace and Princess Frederick had always been right about a natural affinity between the Prince and me. The Prince held me momentarily, not by his easy grasp but by the remarkable power of his eyes. I was vaguely aware of a buzz around us in the big station and guessed that our little meeting was being preserved for tabloid posterity.

"The so-beautiful Kay Amberley, at last!" His Highness murmured in English. "*Ma mère* said you were pretty. Absurd to say you were merely pretty. You agree, Gustaf?"

"A person of rare loveliness," Comte Gustaf von Stieff graciously agreed, and in other circumstances I would like to have asked the poor man what else he could do but agree with his august ruler's son, the heir to the principality?

From these first promising minutes until my return to my elaborate apartments in the Palace at three the next morning, I had no time to mope around, wasting my life on useless self-examination. Looking back on that night and those that followed during the weeks of the

Jubilee, with all our activity played out against a fairy-land of music, bands, Grand Balls, decorations, ribbons, banners and all the trappings of a Graustark, I know that in many ways they were the most enjoyable of my life. For one thing, I was one of the few friends and royal guests of Her Highness who had no title, beyond that mercenary one tacked onto me by the press. When the European newsmen and photographers prowled along after us, exposing our expensive foibles such as the Masquerade for the *Weiburg Hôpital des Enfants* at which we wore costumes of gold or silver and precious stones, I was only one of many condemned by the Leftist Press for "taking money out of the mouths of the starving people."

The Princess Frederick said one morning over coffee in her exquisite, if enormous white bedroom, "How well you and Stefan Nicolaievich get on together! He is extremely taken with you."

I found it difficult to talk of the Prince as if, in boasting of his attention, I would suddenly lose him. I had soon learned that his greatest attraction was not his looks but his charm which I found irresistible. He was warm and gay upon every occasion when we met and though he had flirted with me publicly the first night of my stay at Feldenstein, he made love to me with words and sneaking but not unwelcome kisses without ever getting down to the serious business of trying to get me to bed with him. I found it a refreshing, if challenging change from my experience with past lovers.

He seemed much younger and, of course, less sombre than Luc Sebastiani in his approach to life. This suited me very well, as I wanted to make no mental comparisons between the two men. My feeling for Stefan was light, cheerful, delightful. No deep and painful thoughts about him troubled me. The whole tenor of my life changed and lifted. As I sat talking with the Princess that morn-

185

ing near the end of the Jubilee Celebration, I tried to explain just how I reciprocated her son's feelings, while still being honest as to their degree.

"He makes me feel happy. He raises my spirits. And yet he can speak intelligently on any subject. What he arouses in me is so different from the awful pain and longing I . . ." At Her Highness' penetrating look, I broke off quickly and rephrased what I was about to add, placing it in the past tense. ". . . the longing I once thought I must feel for the man I loved."

She stirred her pale *café au lait* and was about to drink, then changed her mind and said before she did so, "I rather suspect it is better that all the loves in one's life are not equally painful. Nicolas Frederick, who was the father of Stefan Nicolaievich, caused me very little pain; since our mutual feeling was one of respect and a shared and sacred interest in the governing of our country. We were cousins, as you probably know. Believe me, my dear Kay, such a foundation for a marriage is far more comfortable than burning passions."

I smiled. By daylight, and with the prospect of lovely, happy excursions accompanied by a witty and charming male companion, I found it easy to agree with the Princess. It was only upon occasion, and alone in my huge canopied royal bed at night, that my body and all my senses burned for a remembered love.

Luc . . . do you think of me sometimes? Do you ever remember and re-live as I do, those few widely spaced meetings with me?

I knew something of his present activities. He had intended to come to the Jubilee with his wife, Princess Frederick said, but at the last minute the Princess suggested that the climate might be a bit rainy for Claire who was recuperating from a long siege of acute anemia. So, at the Princess' hint, Luc took Claire to Marbella on the Southern Spanish coast instead. He was still the Number One of the Cortot Team but he raced seldom now. He was working with Cortot on safety features for the regular output of Cortot manufactured motors. I found myself trembling with secret relief at this news. At least, I would not have to live the ultimate horror in our unfulfilled relationship, picking up the newspaper casually to read of his flaming death on some faraway track.

The Prince burst open both tall, gold-panelled doors of his mother's sitting room, leaving a startled lackey in elegant gold-edged gray uniform to close the doors respectfully behind him.

Stefan called halfway across the long room, "Kay, you are late. I suppose *ma mère* is teaching you a great many dull future duties. It is quite unnecessary."

"What is all this, *cheri?*" asked the Princess, presenting her cheek for his kiss. "Why unnecessary?"

"Because Kay will have but one duty. To please me!" His looks, his manner always dazzled me, and yet they made me laugh too, because he seemed so happy and well-balanced.

"I beg Your Highness' pardon," I put in to the Princess while pretending to avoid her son's teasing pursuit of my hand to kiss. "But I am afraid we are talking at cross-purposes. I haven't been asked to perform any duties, personal or public. And I think Your Highnesses both forget I am what they call a commoner."

Stefan Nicolaievich had captured my hand and said over his shoulder to his mother, "No one is ever a commoner who has nearly two billions of dollars. This, my sweet—" to me, "makes you of the highest and most select eligibility. It is only my good fortune, which I confess I deserve, that you are also beautiful."

The Princess glanced at me a bit anxiously. "Really, Stefan! If she were not my dear Grace's niece, she might take your teasing seriously. She has a great deal more to offer than a fortune."

187

But I was not offended by his frankness. I had lived much too long to have any illusions that my fortune could be swept under a rug and forgotten. It was an asset to me, just as an actress' asset might be her aura of fame. There was, I knew perfectly well, a genuine truth in F. Scott Fitzgerald's subtle remark about "Daisy Buchanan's" magic charm, that it was full of money. The one thing I had learned to mistrust and even to despise in those people who were drawn to me, was the pretense that they had never once thought of me in connection with money. Luc Sebastiani might have loved me as a woman, but that woman had become the particular person he loved, with her especial and individual qualities, because she was born an exceedingly rich woman. Since he had loved me as I was, he could hardly love me in the same way if I had been born poor. I would be quite a different person, possibly better, but certainly different.

"*Ma mère*," said the Prince, though his luminous dark eyes were upon me, "I am about to end my long and happy bachelorhood. I have found the woman who can laugh with me. And so very rich, *ma mère*. Think of it, if she chooses, she can buy our little kingdom right out from under us! Not that Feldenstein is worth two billion dollars!"

We all laughed.

The Princess raised her coffee cup in a toast: "To the daughter I have always prayed for. Long live Katharine Nicolaievna von Feldenstein!"

"Long live the Princess Katharine!" Stefan repeated gaily.

I remember thinking how light I felt. How gay and elated! As if I were a little drunk.

FIFTEEN/

I COULD hardly convince either the Princess or Stefan that one should not make plans that would decide one's whole future life in just a handful of weeks. To emphasize my warning I flew home as far as New York, took a notion to open the old Sutton Place apartment and remained there, trying to think, and especially to avoid pressures, pro and con, about the Feldenstein matter. Then the little, insidious tentacles of loneliness crept around me and I compared this hermetic life with the happiness of being wanted that I had felt with Stefan and his mother. And the little country itself needed me. An enchanting place it was, balancing bravely and cleverly on a tight rope between great powers. A country in which I felt I might actively and personally be useful. Through agents, I checked into the financial structure of Feldenstein and found, surprisingly enough, that it was perhaps the only country in the world operating without a huge, budgetary deficit. I felt that while any money and influence I chose to risk there would be appreciated, it was something quite different that the Prince and Princess wanted of me. I thought I had an answer when Mike Stannert flew in from the Coast with a message, "very hush-hush" as he put it, from Mother.

He came direct to Sutton Place, arriving just after my temporary New York staff of cook and cleaning woman had left for the night. Only my maid, Pegeen, slept in, and she was visiting her relatives in Boston that weekend.

"Myra's at one of those Golden Doorway slimming places, getting an overhaul which she frankly dosen't need," Mike told me after he had lifted me clear off the foyer floor to buss me on the forehead like a good stepfather. "Guess what, Kay? Somebody thinks you've got the Black Plague. Or maybe it's only Leprosy."

He had to be kidding, I thought, and dismissed his tantalizing opening remarks. "Never mind that for a minute. Come in and take off that wet slicker. You're dripping on Mrs. Butchard's nicely polished floor."

We walked into the living room together, arm in arm. I was genuinely glad to see him, partly because I was lonesome, and partly too, because he might view the whole thing about Feldenstein in perspective. He fixed us both drinks, flattering me that the much too filmy peignoir and nightgown I was wearing made him feel young again. As he was hardly five years older than I, I said I resented the implication, but we both laughed, and felt amazingly warm, domestic and cozy there, sitting on hassocks before the cheerful little fire in the corner grate.

"It's funny," he remarked thoughtfully after a while, his Irish face illuminated now and then by an unexpected crackle of the fire. "Myra never seems to grow older. You and I do, and the rest of the world, but not Myra."

"Thanks a lot."

"You know what I mean, damn it! You grow more beautiful. More worth a man's effort. More grown up.

190

But Myra still seems like a spoiled, head-tossing teen-ager."

Uneasy, I said nothing to his truth about Mother that I had always known. He swizzled his Scotch around and drank it off. He had tough, very male hands. The light hairs seemed to gleam in the firelight. I wondered how many women there had been in his life since he married Mother.

"How is that darling boy of Chiye's?" I asked suddenly, not to be nasty, but because he would have been, to me, the most precious person I knew.

"The little tyke's almost grown. He's signed up for Hawaii University. Your friend, Ito Shimbashi, is going to tutor him on vacations to fill in at his office. The way I figure it, my kid may end up in Washington yet, as a senator. Imagine, the son of old Mike Stannert, Shanty Irishman!"

I thought it wonderful and said so. But the mention of his boy had reminded him of his errand with me.

"Kay, somebody's sure interested in whether you can have your own kids or not. If you'll pardon the frankness. Every doctor you ever had in Frisco and the Islands has been questioned."

I guessed at once who was investigating my medical reports, and why. It also satisfied a question I had asked myself: what was the Princess' panic about marrying off her son? He had been a happy and internationally known playboy bachelor for so long, it seemed funny that the Princess was now anxious to get him married. But I could see how important it was to the dynasty. Heaven knows what would become of the little country if Princess Frederick and Prince Stefan both died without leaving another heir! With an Iron Curtain country sharing Feldenstein's southeastern border along what was called a 'corridor' of a few kilometres, there might even be international complications.

191

"Never mind. I know who and also why," I said, as we sat comfortably toasting our faces and bodies before the fire. I was dying to ask him if he had heard from Luc, but I didn't like to bring up the subject, for fear he would guess the depths of my interest. Sparks leaped up from the fire, spattering a display of fireworks over the brick hearth and the next minute Mike was beating out the sparks that landed on the filmy material of my peignoir. It was all over in a few seconds with both of us out of breath and laughing as we saw the absurd juxtaposition of Mike's big male hand, caught in the inset lace of my skirt.

"What a hero! You saved my life."

"Really nothing, old girl!"

I helped to untangle his fingers from the lace, still amused. We were both looking down, both suddenly aware of those intangibles that combined between us now, to make a greater danger than the sparks from the fire. For perhaps five seconds, as Mike's hand closed on my thigh and I felt the heat of it through the translucent peignoir, we looked at each other. I felt the quickening of my pulsebeat, the now familiar, maddening warmth that suffused my loins, and when Mike's other hand moved to cup one of my breasts, gently but with a growing urgency that I could guess at, I let him do so, trembling with desire, not for Mike, but for the body of him, the life of him that must possess me, if only briefly. He was no longer Mike Stannert, my mother's husband. He was Karl, and Jacques whom I had lost, and faceless others whose bodies I remembered though their names were forgotten, and he was Luc Sebastiani whom I wanted him to be, most of all. But he was not the Prince. That was strange. Later that night, I wondered why.

Mike began to draw me down to the rug before the hearth. I felt myself sinking, yielding, not to his hands which were big enough and powerful enough to hurt me, but yielding to that awful longing within me.

And then, like some ill-timed second act curtain, the telephone chimed. The spell was broken for me, and I knew that as I struggled painfully to free myself, Mike would eventually be as relieved as I was that we hadn't completed this despicable betrayal. I finally had to bite him to make him let me go. I drew away from him, crawling a few inches across the rug until I could get to my feet and reach for the telephone extension on its little teakwood stand. While I was answering the call, Mike got up, flushed and breathing heavily. I was relieved when he mouthed the words: "Sorry—sort of," grinned and began to straighten out his dishevelled clothing.

As for me, my hands were still palsied from the too-abrupt cutting off of that emotional need so close to being satisfied. My call was from an overseas operator and began with a jumble of French and German followed by Prince Stefan's voice, full of that warmth and light I remembered with pleasure and a surprising homesickness. I wondered how he knew where to find me, but as it turned out, Mother, on the Coast, gave him the number.

"Sweet Katharine, I miss you. When do you return?"

"I miss you too. But I don't know. There are so many things to consider. Meanwhile, Your Highness cannot possibly miss me when I've seen how every female in Europe adores you."

Mike's eyebrows had gone up at Stefan's title and having somewhat recovered his equilibrium, he made faces at me while reaching for his rain slicker. I was relieved that he knew he had to go, and the sooner the better.

"Do not talk about the others, Katharine Nicolaievna. I despise them. I need you. I need only you, very much. More than you know. Come back and let us laugh together."

Although I did not promise, he had without knowing it, said the two things most calculated to sway me. The need for me, and the sense that with him there would be happiness and laughter.

Mike knew. When he was leaving, after I completed the phone call, he said wisely, "The fellow makes you look quite different. He's for you?"

"You mean you can tell I love him? Even I don't know that."

"No, honey." He turned up his coat collar in preparation for the weather. "You've loved before. You might even have loved me. For a few minutes. It's not that, old girl. It's something else you need more. And don't make the mistake of trading it in for what you call—'love.'"

I didn't understand him, but I liked him for saying it. "Say hello to Mother for me. If she ever gives you trouble, tell her she's lucky. You love her."

He looked back over his shoulder. His face was in shadow. "That's where you got off the track a long time ago, Kay. I've loved a lot of women. But it's Myra who needs me. Remember that with your Highness guy. You're like me, in a lot of ways. You have to be needed. And he needs you like Myra needs me. That'll hold two people together a hell of a lot longer than sex!"

When he was gone, I went and curled up on the rug by the warm hearth and it seemed to me that the darkening coals, with their heart of fire, glowed for me like the eyes of Stefan Nicolaievich. I decided to call him and the Princess in the morning. The decision gave me peace. I felt rested and happy.

My very first congratulatory cablegram on the Court Announcement of our engagement came to me in Weiburg from Mother.

"You make me proud of you. You have at last fulfilled your potential," is how she put it. Hildy put it a bit differently: "Hi, Princess! Hope the glass slipper fits. Love

194

and Curtseys from Hildy the American." I imagine this was as subtly as Hildy could express it that no prince was worth trading away my citizenship. She did not know that this very problem caused me my deepest concern until I discovered that my oath to support and defend the Royal House of Feldenstein could be expressed in such a way as to preclude my giving up my United States citizenship. I have always suspected that the enormous tax burden of the Amberley corporate structure, or at least that part of it incorporated in American states, helped to ease the way for me in the matter of retaining a double citizenship. It was implicit in my act of marriage however, as in the Roman Catholic Service itself, that my children were to be reared not only in their father's faith but of his nationality; since they would be next in line of succession, after Stefan Nicolaievich. I began to take instruction in the state religion from Feldenstein's Archbishop Mihailoff. More than any other preparation, this showed me the solemnity of my undertaking.

My own future name seemed extraordinarily hard to get used to: Katharine Nicolaievna von Feldenstein, and when *Paris Match* did a surprisingly good picture spread of preparations for the Royal Wedding, as it was called, I began to believe that for once in my life I had achieved dignity in the public prints. It was not true, of course. Almost immediately, a West German scandal sheet and an American monthly that ran a fine line between legality and defamation, came out with exposés of "The Playgirl Life of Golden Kay, the World's Richest Woman." It was sickening to see all my mistakes and past stupidity, spread out before me, so that I relived the shameful business of Jacques Levescu and the honeymoon stops from Tijuana to San Francisco, as well as other men I had slept with during the Jet years. All the Golden Kay promiscuity was there, with my conduct hinted at, and the cutting addition, "Now Golden Kay has bought herself a prince. Will this latest purchase bring her happiness at last? Or will she go on searching, purchasing, discarding, or being discarded when money can no longer be wrung from the still-lovely woman we used to call the luckiest, the richest girl in the world?"

It made me feel dirty all over. And sick. I thought that long ago I had shed my last tears, that I was hardened and insulated by the repetition of such painful experiences in my life, but here it was again and hurting as much as ever. I wanted to shred the pages of the magazine and stuff them down the editor's throat. Meanwhile, I found myself crying silently, and my hands unable to do their job of ripping up the pages. Before the magazines were laid on my desk by the furious Pegeen who then left me alone in my sitting room, I had been memorizing my own part in the complicated ritual of the religious wedding. The civil service was much simpler and would take place the day before the ceremony in the Weiburg St. Mihail Cathedral. But my mood was wrecked and I felt terribly depressed, for the first time during the months I had spent in Feldenstein learning what I thought must be my real life's role.

I felt a hand on my shoulder and I moved nervously. I had thought I was alone. The most disconcerting thing about Palace life, I found, was the goldfish bowl it made of one's privacy. I looked up while trying unobtrusively to locate a handkerchief. I failed, and saw the Prince gazing down at me with that warm sympathy which, in my experience, always made my tears brim over.

"I hope it is not the prospect of the wedding that makes you so sad, Katharine, my Kate." But he could see at once what brought on my depression and his free hand pushed it angrily onto the floor. "Do not think about it. The past, and the lies, they do not matter. So long as you can love me."

"As long as I could love him". . . . What a curious

196

thing to say, when he could have his choice of any eligible noblewoman in the world! I said this out loud and to my surprise he laughed so much I forgot all about my gloom and began to find his good humor contagious. We laughed together. I still didn't know why, nor did I know why he thought it amusing when I said he might have his choice of any eligible woman in the world. He was much too sophisticated to believe he was unattractive.

"Well then, if you don't think of it, I won't," I promised and, as his face approached much closer, I raised up a little and kissed his pale, olive cheek. His friendship, and even his very sincere liking for me I didn't doubt. I supposed I had been merely the least repulsive of the marriage prospects paraded before him. I couldn't forget how often in the past he and I had managed to avoid meeting each other. For these reasons I was more than touched. I loved him for his next gesture. He touched the flesh very gently beneath my eyes with one finger and then, as I started at the feathery touch, he said, barely above a whisper, before he kissed me, "Thank you for agreeing with all of *ma mère's* plots and schemes. Thank you, because I need you." We kissed. I felt none of the hot passion aroused in me by Luc or even Karl. Instead, I felt a warm, strong happiness, a well-being such as I could never remember feeling before.

It was all very strange, and with each day, as I learned more of my duties, more of what was expected of me, the peculiarly rigid etiquette upon certain occasions, the reserve of feeling in public, I found always the mystery about my future husband. I saw him less than I might have expected, and began to guess that the pallor of his, and the darkness of his eyes, his slenderness, the fact that I never saw him in any athletic endeavor, not tennis, or racing or dancing, or even stiff walks, all suggested he was not as well as I had been led to believe. I hated to ask Stefan himself about his health, though upon several occasions I almost broached the subject, when I had not seen him all day and when, as I strongly suspected, he was suffering during the minutes we were together at a state banquet. But in spite of these times, when my hints to his mother for information were avoided, I had full days in Stefan's company, and these were the best times. I was astonished afterward to realize how much we had in common and how happy I felt after twelve or fourteen hours alone with him. Our disagreements were the kind that a smile or a simple word of reasonable understanding settled in no time. There were none of the uneasy silences that had upset me in my relationships with lovers in my past. I seemed to have with Stefan none of the self-consciousness, the deep suffering and craving for sensuous fulfillment that I had known in my youth. And we had much in common in our backgrounds. Stefan had been reared, as I was, in the aura of a unique label, in my case, the richest girl in the world. In the international press, Stefan's label, so ironic in view of my later knowledge, was that of the most eligible bachelor in the world, and the handsomest prince.

He seemed to delight in my company as I delighted in his. We laughed at small things. We found that life was at its best over these very minutes and hours with the simple clasp of the hands, or a kiss on the lips while we fought happily over the last drop of champagne in a silver picnic decanter.

As it happened, I discovered the truth about my fiancé from an old, familiar informant. It was two days before Mother and Mike were flying in with Ann and Morgan Haight and Hildy. Mother never hit it off well with Hildy; so Ann had promised to act as a buffer between them. When my early morning tea was brought to my sitting room, I found a small, scented and very feminine envelope beside the Paris and Zurich newspapers. I ripped it open with the small butter knife monogrammed for the Royal Family. Although I couldn't recall having seen Claire Sebastiani's handwriting, the tone of the letter was so obviously hers:

"Cherie, how good to know you are in Feldenstein! Luc and I are near Weiburg, Luc to put the new Cortot Claire through trial runs, and I to repair a small but annoying problem of the blood. I note you are to marry an old friend of mine, Stefan Nicolaievich. Do come and see me this morning at the Sanitorium south of the capital. You will find it worth your while. I suggest you do not mention your visit to Their Highnesses quite yet.

"Je vous embrasse affecteusement,
Claire Sebastiani."

. . . This is bound to be unpleasant, I thought, and I nearly ignored the letter with its none too subtle command. I wonder what path my life would have taken today if I really had ignored her letter. After some quarrels with myself over yielding so easily to Claire's needling, I changed from the over-elaborate gray velvet dressing gown with gold satin ribbons given to me by the Princess, into the first outfit I could reach which happened to be one of my Chanel trousseau suits. I reflected momentarily that it was supposed to be bad luck for the wedding if I wore it beforehand, but I wanted to get the unpleasantness of Claire over and done with.

Two Feldenstein women of noble families had been chosen as my Ladies-in-Waiting, necessary to my position after the wedding, as Her Highness put it, and, of course, I met them now in one of the huge palace corridors as I hurried out to the Porsche I had bought sight unseen, a week before and which I still was trying to tame. I made excuses to the women, which were palpable lies, and the two ladies glanced at each other significantly. I was sure they thought I was on my way to meet a secret lover. Cu-

199

riously enough, I had not thought of meeting the only man I could ever think of as my secret lover. Everything I read between the lines of Claire's note told me that Luc knew nothing about her invitation, nor did she expect me to meet him there. It was, I knew, an invitation to an unpleasantness 'between us girls', but if I did not go, some calamity would undoubtedly befall me, and perhaps Stefan, when it was too late. In considering this aspect, I discovered with surprise that for the first time since my naïve adoration of Jacques Levescu, I cared as much for Stefan's happiness as for my own. His gaiety, his gentleness, his need of me, and lately his understanding of my own unhappiness, had gotten to me in a way I never thought possible after my long journey from naïve Kay Levescu to sophisticated, imperturbable Kay Dorn.

I thought deeply of my responsibilities to the little country and its rulers, as I drove through the city with its fresh, golden and gray decorations for my own wedding to their prince, driving under the improvised coronets of wire and gold cloth, past flapping royal standards with the ancient Carolingian quarterings. I came out, at last, upon the highway south. While I was occupied with uneasy imaginings, wondering what Claire Sebastiani had planned with which to surprise me, I also gave some thought to the Amberley corporate structure in America, relieved that our careful planning after Aunt Grace's death had divided the Amberley octopus so that no one monolithic giant like Grace Evelina Amberley would ever again be necessary. Men who had worked with Aunty and for her during the past fifty years were now performing admirably as heads of the many new enterprises, funds, charities, hospitals and internationally founded colleges. While I would be flying back to America every two or three months to be briefed on my own interests, it had become obvious to me that I was not, personally, indispensable to the Amberley octopus; whereas, I might become indispensable to my husband and to this little country which was rapidly capturing my heart. It was, I thought, the one combination of circumstances that had finally overshadowed my long, adulterous passion for Luc Sebastiani.

After avoiding numerous bicyclists on their way into Weiburg, and an overturned, apparently abandoned tumbrel of new hay, I reached the Sanitorium quicker than I had expected to. I was surprised at its elegance, the enchanting miniature forest that added to its low-roofed, cottage atmosphere. If one must be sick, it was the place to be sick. I discovered that I was expected, which gave me a new respect for Claire Sebastiani's self-confidence.

I was ushered through wide, airy halls to a cheerful room whose two windows, now closed, looked out upon vistas of greenery still dripping from an early morning shower. Within this atmosphere of spring and renewed life, it was a frightful shock to see Claire Sebastiani as she looked, sitting on a *chaise longue,* but wrapped up to her throat in a satin-quilted comforter. Her thin, fragile face was like a beautifully moulded skull, the flesh transparent and its color dominated by the blue of the surface veins. When she raised her skeletal hand to me languidly, I had to swallow hard to hide my feelings; for no matter what jealousies and dislikes I had experienced over her in the past, I could see that she was a dying woman, and the presence of this death carried a contagious horror.

"*Bonjour, chérie,* and congratulations. You have made a remarkable purchase. A fully accredited prince." Her golden eyes were narrow, regarding me with amusement.

I got hold of myself, answering her in kind, with an equally false smile. "In America, I believe it is customary to congratulate the prospective groom and to wish the bride happiness."

"But, of course, we are not in America; isn't it so?" She tried to plump up the pillow behind the small of her back, but the effort was too much for her and I reached around to attend to the matter. "Thank you," she said, the skull's face illuminated by the quick, bright smile that must be heartbreaking to those who loved her. "Many thanks . . . Golden Kay . . . Healthy Kay . . . Lucky Kay. How I used to envy you! Did you know that? I'd have sold my soul to have your life, your fortune, your luck. And all I had to bargain with was one thing that you wanted." She looked up at me, her eyes unreadable, with that wise, knowing feline stillness. "I wonder what he would have been worth to you, in dollar currency."

Although her taunts and their underlying truths depressed me terribly, I was surprised at the calm with which I received the news that, long ago, I might have bought off Claire's rights to her husband. I looked around quickly, anxious that Luc should not overhear these disillusioning truths we were discussing. Claire understood, at once.

"Do not worry. He is talking with my physicians. Marbella did not work too well for me, and Luc believes the Swiss clinic may be the answer." She shivered, and I felt again a deep, painful sympathy with the dying woman. "But all one sees for months are the snowy summits. I prefer the greenery here." The dreadful smile glowed fitfully. "I always look my best in green, you know."

I glanced out at the dripping branches that clawed faintly against the window and I blinked. As I would not want my enemies weeping with pity for me, so I did not want to depress her, by the sight of my tears for her. I was about to clear my throat and ask why she had written the note when she brought up the subject abruptly.

"You have probably been told that I spent some time in clinics for one thing or another, and I felt that in all fairness you should know one of my ailments is a form of anemia that you call 'pernicious', I believe. Naturally, I have often met other patients with similar blood complaints."

"Naturally," I agreed, wondering with a heaviness and dread, what she was leading up to.

Her fingers picked at the tufted threads on the comforter. "Long before my marriage, when I was a girl, in fact, I met an exceedingly handsome boy at one of those Swiss clinics which was endowed by Princess Sophie-Frederick. It was said that the boy had a form of anemia like my own." She looked up at me with a quick, sharp movement that was shocking in itself. "But that was not true. You see, I happened to discover, by a little effort, that Prince Stefan-Nicolaievich was suffering from quite a different ailment of the blood. Does it give you a clue if I say that Her Highness, his mother, is twice related to the English Queen Victoria's Prussian descendants?"

In a haze of confusion which overlay the dark horror of these moments, I managed to say finally, "Prince Stefan is a hemophiliac?"

"Small wonder that his mother is so anxious to marry him away from the few remaining royal houses of Europe, eh, chérie? These blood secrets are always known by others who may have the same problem dormant in one generation, but not the next. Now," she added pleasantly, "I think you will re-consider this glamorous marriage of yours."

SIXTEEN/

I BEGAN to move around the room. I couldn't seem to stop my restless pacing. The dangers of that terrible and infinitely painful disease were vaguely known to me. One fact of which I was sure: the disease was transmitted through the female line, and for that reason, any children of Stefan's and mine would not be cursed in that way. But I thought over my past relationship with Feldenstein's royal family, as well as the mystery of the handsome, eligible prince's long bachelorhood, and his frequent disappearances from public notice. It began to fit together. What a terrible prison of suspense and fear and pain Stefan must live in! And I had remarked on his marvelous optimism, his cheerfulness and gaiety!

Claire was watching me with keen interest, reading many things in my face that were quite opposed to her clever conclusions:

"It makes a difference; does it not?"

I heard a nurse speaking in German in the corridor and I lowered my voice to ask without any expression, "Why did you tell me now?"

"For money," she said airily. "You wish my husband. I am an obstacle. For one million dollars paid to me at once and in negotiable quantities, I will divorce Luc. And live out the rest of my life as I have always dreamed. A rich woman."

The irony of this was so terrible I found it difficult to keep her from guessing my pity. Obviously, she did not know that she was dying.

"Is it not worth one of those paltry millions of yours, to have the man who loves you free to marry you?"

"How do you know Luc loves me?"

"*Chérie,* I may be a trifle tired at the moment, but I am not blind. He reads every word that appears about his Golden Kay. He was depressed for weeks when the rumors began about you and poor Stefan. As for me," she took a long, obviously painful breath, looking off toward the doorway, behind me. "I knew long ago that he was the love of your young life."

It seemed to me as she uttered this truth I had lived with for ten years, that the words aroused nothing at all in me, no emotion except the realization that six months ago I would have felt hot and guilty and embittered at the mention of this fact. Right now, my emotions were stunned by two far greater facts: this dying woman, and the tragic secret in the life of the happiest man I had ever known. Her intent stare over my shoulder made me turn abruptly, as I sensed that we were being overheard. A nurse who stood in the doorway, in her stiff white nun's habit, was looking away from us, along the corridor.

"*Bitte, Frau Sebastiani,* is it *Herr Sebastiani* who has been here a moment ago? He did not sign with the nurse on duty."

Claire's thin fingers waved at her in a little gesture of dismissal. "It was not my husband. Do not concern yourself. My husband is with the Administrator and my physicians."

"But the gentleman I thought I saw. . . ."

". . . was not Luc. I do not need you yet, Sister Ritter. Perhaps, when Madame and I have completed our visit."

I pulled myself together, still stunned by my two discoveries, and started toward the door. The nurse looked me up and down and suddenly recognized me. She started to curtsey, but the gesture shook me so much I pleaded with her almost hysterically, "No, please!"

Meanwhile, the pitiful, skull's face of Claire Sebastiani was turned upward to me and her voice, for the first time, showed panic. The thought of it, the feel of it, twisted my heart.

"*Chérie*—you have not answered my offer. A deal, I believe you would call it. We make a deal for my—my merchandise. No?"

I wanted to tell her that she would have her million, or whatever she needed to give her perfect care and as much happiness as any human being can absorb, who bases it solely upon the possession of more money than she can live to spend. But I wanted nothing from her in return. And I hoped that Luc would never know of her 'deal'. I had one objective now, to return to those two, the Princess and Stefan, who needed and counted on me, and whom I had needed all my life, though I hadn't known it. How strange and remarkable that a man under daily sentence of death should offer me so much charm and laughter and, in his own way, love!

The nurse tried to stop me, hesitantly. "Frau Sebastiani asks Your Highness a question, I believe."

"I know. And I am not Her Highness for another week." But I looked back at Claire, trying to conceal my horror and my pity, a pity I would never feel for Stefan, because he deserved so much more. "All right, Claire. Don't worry about the deal. You'll have everything you can possibly want."

206

She raised up painfully on the *chaise*. The nurse hurried to help her. "And—Luc?"

"I never deal in human beings." I left them and hurried along the corridor. As I reached the little glass enclosure of the nurse on reception duty, she looked across the counter at me.

"Oh, Frau Dorn! You are alone. Then you missed him?"

"Missed who?" I asked, assuming that she referred to Luc whom Nurse Ritter thought she had seen in the doorway of his wife's room. I wondered what my own feelings would be when I met Luc again. For a very few seconds today I had considered what it would be like to be completely amoral, to accept the deal Claire offered. But even if there were no Stefan, Claire's dying gesture of greed would always stand between us. And there was Stefan.

The receptionist looked puzzled.

"His Serene Highness, *bitte*. Prince Stefan came in shortly ago, very agitated. He said your ladies saw you leave, and he had come to drive you back to the palace. He went to Frau Sebastiani's room. Did he leave?"

This, then, was the truth of those seconds when someone stood behind me in the doorway of Claire's room. Nurse Ritter had seen Prince Stefan, not Luc, and so had Claire. She must have talked about Luc's love for me deliberately, knowing the Prince overheard it. What had happened to him? How would Claire's cruel news affect him? I began to run, past the receptionist, into the foyer. A nurse called after me, "You look for His Highness? He has gone to his car. He did not look well, Madame. Very pale and excited. Quite shocking. He would not stop when I spoke."

Frantic now, I cried, "Help me to stop him, someone. Please? *Bitte?*" I pushed open one of the outside doors and hurried down the steps.

On the driveway below two men stood with their hands on the open door of a low, sleek, green sports car that looked rather like a vicious green shark. The man facing me was Stefan. He seemed as lighthearted as I would always remember him. He was laughing, yet persistent about something. The morning breeze carried a speckle of mist, and together, they whipped a tendril of black hair across his forehead. Except for his usual pallor, he looked healthier than the older Luc Sebastiani, whose lean, hard profile and body I recognized at once as those of the other man.

In spite of Stefan's appearance of easy humor, I could tell from Luc's voice that the argument between them was passionate and angry, at least on Luc's part.

"I must forbid it, Your Highness. I know I promised you, but that is for a time when you are accompanied by a professional, and not in your present mood."

"Now! My friend, I insist!" There was an odd, stubborn fixity to Stefan's cheerful insistence. He saw me as he spoke, and raised his voice for my benefit. "You see? Katharine expects it. Come. Be a good fellow. Katharine, I'll show you I can do anything Luc can do with a car!"

Luc swung around, taking his hand away from the car door as Stefan mentioned my name.

"Kay, talk sense to His Highness. This car is experimental. It is not ready yet for amateurs."

I was running toward the two men when Stefan, behind the wheel, slammed the door and the heavy roar of the motor startled both Luc and me. As the low, green car leaped forward, the stencilled name on the door blurred before my eyes: CORTOT CLAIRE.

. . . . She loves green, I remembered. And did she deliberately do this to Stefan, as well? Does she want to take someone with her on her journey?

I cried to Stefan to stop, but the car rushed past me

with that hideous, heavy roar of the motor, and I caught a flash of Stefan's hand saluting me. Behind me the receptionist screamed. I turned and ordered her sharply, "Call Her Highness or the Chancellor. Tell them what has happened." I hoped against hope that at least Stefan's mother had arrangements, in case of any accident to him, the readiness of plasma, the instant service of physicians who knew his case.

"Can't you stop him?" I begged Luc as we met. I had forgotten our last meetings, forgotten everything about our old relationship except that he knew Stefan, knew his habits, his condition, and could be of use now. "Is the car hard to handle?"

"Difficult, but not impossible for the Prince," Luc said, taking my arm. "Have you a key to the Porsche?" I stared at him. "The key, darling. The key!"

As he hurried me along the gravel drive, I fumbled for my key ring and gave it to him. Everything afterward happened in a burst of speed and panic. My fear for Stefan was balanced by Luc's calm, icy control. The Porsche took off nearly as rapidly and noisily as the Cortot Claire. In the distance, at the end of the tree-lined drive, we could see the sleek, sharklike Cortot Claire zoom into the main highway, headed for town.

"It's suicidal!" I muttered, not very coherently, but Luc understood me. He kept looking ahead at the junction of private estate road and the highway which was coming up fast, and I could see the tautness of his jaw, the concentration in his whole body, that had been schooled to this sort of tension for so long. One of his hands touched and covered mine briefly, to give me strength.

"There is very little we can do," he reminded me. "The *Polizei*, perhaps, and the First Aid. We can only hope the Palace will act correctly. But we must keep him in sight, if he should need us. What caused this? Was it something she said?"

I was almost startled enough to take my eyes off the road. "How did you know?"

"I guessed. He mentioned beating me back to town. Something about the way he said it. He felt he must prove something to you."

"Yes. Claire told me about Stefan."

He swung out onto the highway. Far in the distance, as it rounded a turn and was hidden by a grove of poplars, we lost sight of the Cortot Claire momentarily.

"Ah. Was that all she told you?" he asked me then, glancing quickly at me and away. There was very little auto traffic, but several bicyclists suddenly scattered across the road ahead of us like frightened ants and it took all Luc's skill to avoid hitting most of them. They were mostly well-dressed men, peddling to their jobs or their business, or perhaps to see the decorations for the Royal Wedding.

I found myself using Stefan's name in a prayer, feeling my hands icy as they pressed upon my eyes in my panic. And then, loudly, I cried, "He doesn't really know how I feel. You see, he thinks—" I couldn't go on, and I couldn't betray Luc's wife.

Luc's quiet voice had its good effect upon me. "He will know finally. He is a good driver. There are so many things he would be good at, but for that cursed blood thing. It has always been remarkable to me that his illness hasn't embittered him as Claire's illness embittered her. I can't blame Claire, but your husband-to-be is a remarkable person."

"The slightest injury could kill him; couldn't it? Don't you understand?"

"I understand very well. My . . . Kay. I saw him nearly bleed to death once. In Manzanares, years ago.

210

Someone bet him he couldn't last one hundred seconds in the training ring with a rather nasty specimen of bull. He lasted. But he skinned one leg, getting back over the fence. That was all. One leg skinned. An hour later, he was in excruciating pain. The swelling of the joints, and the pockets of bleeding, I will never forget."

And yet Stefan laughed a great deal, and was always so cheerful! Perhaps he had found laughter the only way to preserve his sanity at the horror of his ever-present danger.

"How can we stop him? Or see that he isn't hurt. How?"

"I don't know. I cannot take the chance of giving him a close race, if we could catch him up. And the Cortot has too much power. I know."

"Then, maybe he will make it to town safely."

"Maybe, but that car is not a plaything." He slapped the wheel over hard and I did not dare to speak again until he had maneuvered the low-slung car onto a badly paved, rutted road that seemed to be the original, abandoned highway. The road leaped over low, rolling hills from which we could see the spires of St. Mihail Cathedral, the rooftops of Weiburg and the broad, Romanesque front of the Palace itself. I could see now why Luc had taken this road in spite of the difficulty the low Porsche had in getting over the ruts and humps. It was possible to keep the speeding green Cortot always in sight on the highway below us. Our own road wound around the hill, down to the remnants of the ancient Roman wall encircling the heart of the city. Just before the new highway entered the outskirts of the city I made out the overturned tumbrel of what looked like green hay that I had passed on my outward run. It was surrounded by observers, many on bicycles, and by Feldenstein road police in their gray uniforms with their flashing white lights that signalled at either end of the wreck. The horse who had been dragging the load stood patiently in a field opposite, considering the whole wreck as if it had no connection with him.

Luc raced along, putting out all the power of which the car was capable, and I guessed that he wanted to be at the scene of the wreck if possible before Stefan. It seemed that we might make it; we were closer, but the sleek green Cortot was incredibly fast. I could only hope Stefan would see the evidence of the overturned cart, and the surrounding crowd soon enough so that he could have time to slow down the unfamiliar car. A motorcyclist in the uniform of the Road Police was racing out of town, and as we rattled down the hill we saw the motorcyclist stop to speak with the police at the wreck. They seemed to be expecting him, and one of them started off with him on a second motorcycle toward the distant, approaching Cortot Claire.

"They must have been warned to make it appear a normal road warning," Luc said, taking his eyes off the bumpy road long enough to glance toward Stefan's car. Seconds later, we began to hear the shrill, wobbling sound of the police klaxons and as we reached the highway, Stefan's car was still out of sight, hidden from us by the slope of the hill. All traffic in the area of the overturned tumbrel was motionless and as we also came to a brief standstill, we could hear the roar of distant motors, the cycles' sharp warning, and Luc, staring in that direction murmured, "The Cortot is slowing. If he can handle it now, through this crowd. . . ."

The green streak roared into sight around the hill. Even I could see that Stefan had managed to bring the motor down to a speed he could control in another few seconds, but in those seconds a female bicyclist loomed up out of nowhere, wending her way across the highway. While the police screamed at her, motioning her over to

212

the roadside, the Cortot cleared the debris of the tumbrel, braking skillfully as I watched with a numbness almost beyond fear.

"Good lad!" Luc exclaimed. "Easy . . . easy. . . ."

But the bicyclist, confused by the police orders, lost her balance and fell over into the road just as Stefan was bringing the Cortot to a halt. He swerved away from the cyclist with a split second to spare, and came to a rocking stop on the apron of the road. Luc and I were out of our car and stumbling across the intervening ground toward the Cortot Claire almost before its momentum died. Police and bystanders hurried after us. I could hear the thud of boots over the ground but all these sounds and impressions faded before the one overwhelming sight of Stefan pushing the car door open, waving to us in tired triumph.

"Thank God!" Luc muttered. "He seems to have come out of it without a single scratch."

Knowing the effect of a "single scratch" on Stefan, I kept silent, wanting only to reassure myself by a closer sight of him. Stefan hadn't gotten out of the car yet, but I could tell by his glance from me to Luc that he was trying to decide what there was between us, whether his childish and near-disastrous effort to show off had made an impression on me. It had! Possibly the most important impression of my life.

He was just starting to slide out of the car when I reached him. We embraced as I had recently been taught we must never do in public, and Stefan challenged me, "Well then, Katharine, what did you think of that little run?"

Neither of us was aware that Luc had gone around the green Cortot and gotten in beside Stefan, until he said quietly, "May I drive Your Highness into town?"

We both turned to stare at him. Then, as Stefan winced

213

at an unsuspected pain, and jerked away his right arm self-consciously, I saw the thing that gave Luc his tense expression and his insistence. There was a smear of blood on the elbow of Stefan's topcoat. It had already soaked through the thick tweed. He murmured in the most polite but authoritative way, "Please . . . say nothing. They must not know. But you are right. We had better hurry."

SEVENTEEN/

The long anguish of waiting taught me as much about myself as about Princess Frederick who shared my vigil, and to whom this must represent one more nightmare in a lifetime of torment. She sat very still in a stiff milord chair in the Prince's study, leaning forward, with her fingers laced tightly together, and she stared unseeing, at the pattern in the Aubusson carpet. I kept getting up and then sitting down, doing a great deal of walking, all in the confines of that warm, masculine, leathery room that was Stefan's unofficial office for the paper work of his position. My nervousness must have been especially difficult for the Princess to bear, but she was understanding enough not to let me know.

"Why?" I cried finally, stopping in front of her. "There must be something to do, after all these years. Some medicines, some miracle drug. . . . Something! I'd solve it if it cost every cent in the world."

She looked up at me, and she smiled, a smile that was world-weary and knowing.

"My poor child! You still believe that everything in

215

life, even death, may be purchased by the richest girl in the world."

I was stunned by her reminder. It stopped me in the middle of my helpless protest against life's cruelties, those inequitable cruelties for which I had always, in my ignorance, supposed there must be an explanation. I sank down on my knees before the Princess and touched her tired, stiffened fingers, borrowing strength and even hope.

"He must recover! He will . . . won't he?"

Her hands, freed of their tension, passed over my head, smoothing my hair back tenderly, as though I were a child.

"Yes, he will recover this time. Everything was done quickly. We are always prepared. We must thank God for such all important weapons as plasma, and the new drugs. It was not always so, for my ancestors. Believe me. Already, the hemorrhaging has been stopped. Soon, he will be very much his happy self."

To me, this only meant that Stefan's life blood was no longer draining away. His mother explained to me the excruciating pain suffered before this all-important stoppage of the bleeding, the reasons for the pain, the "pockets of blood" as she called them, that gathered within the joints, around the bone and marrow.

I wasn't aware that I was crying as I listened to her, until the Princess smiled and said to me exactly as Aunt Grace would have done, "It is not correct etiquette to sniff in my presence."

I begged pardon and feeling encouraged by her optimism, confessed, "It is His Highness' happy influence upon me that made me discover I loved him."

"And do you love him, my dear?"

"Oh, yes! Do you think I want to rush in to see him the minute I am permitted, just to cheer him up?"

216

"I certainly hope . . ." She paused, studied me closely. "Why then do you wish to see him?"

"Because I feel miserable when I am not with him. He makes me care for life."

"Possibly because he knows its value."

No one knew it better, I learned, as she talked then of her husband, Prince Nicolas-Frederick von Feldenstein, and told me that she had committed a deep wrong in not explaining the truth of Stefan's disease to me.

"I'm glad you did not tell me," I said then, considering how nearly I might never have met Stefan. "You see, if you had told me, and I had been cowardly, and never come to your Silver Jubilee, I would never have found the deepest happiness I've ever known."

"Thank you, Katharine. Grace was sure you would feel this way. But it was I who was cowardly, and I let you become engaged under false pretenses. Stefan said it would not matter to you. How right he was!" She hesitated, then went on with what, in anyone else, would have been timidity. "It is not my wish to pry. My son believes your past loves are forgotten. I wonder if they are."

I was astonished that she should doubt. I started to say so and found there were no words. The room, despite all its comfortable leathery warmth, seemed stifling because I wanted to prove something and did not know how. Yet, I had no doubts at all, now, unlike the passionate fury with which I had defended my past marriages and my 'great love' as I once called my memories of Luc Sebastiani. I said abruptly, "You ask me if my past loves are forgotten. Claire Sebastiani is dying . . ." I broke off, wondering how to express this.

"And nothing concerning her death affects you?" she asked.

"Nothing but pity. I am sorry for anyone who suffers and dies."

"And Luc's freedom?"

I stared into the unlighted fireplace, trying to analyze my thoughts. "I feel that, to me, at least, he will always belong to Claire."

She nodded. "You grow in wisdom, my dear."

I looked around and asked the Princess why Stefan was treated in his own bedroom suite in the Palace, rather than at a hospital, and the minute she mentioned the first of the series of injuries which had resulted in these agonizing days of struggle, suffering, and temporary relief, I realized the wisdom of having his refuge here where no explanations need be given about his inexplicable disappearances from time to time.

When Stefan was permitted a second visitor, after his mother, I saw him sitting up in a chair with only his arm in a sling and looking, at first glance, very much the way he always looked. Lines of pain had temporarily aged and blurred his remarkable features but his small injury and the enormous ordeal that had followed did not really essentially change him. He stood up to kiss me and then we both went and sat together on a couch and I reminded him, "I'm afraid my mother will be arriving today. I wish it might be later, when—"

He grinned. "—when I have more strength for it, you mean? Is she that much of an ogress, a typical mother-in-law?"

"She is far too beautiful to be an ogress, but I'm afraid she is a typical mother-in-law."

"I promise faithfully not to be seduced by her."

We sat there contentedly holding hands, I with my head against his uninjured shoulder, and he asked me with a quietness that warned me of its importance, "Has Luc left the Palace?"

"He left sometime early yesterday. I'm afraid we didn't notice, your mother and I."

218

"He was very good to me. He did not get angry when I nearly wrecked his car. And stole his girl."

We looked at each other.

"I believe you did, at that," I admitted, with all my love in my eyes. "At least, I know what you overheard Claire say yesterday was a lie. For my part, I know it was a lie."

"Poor Claire. We have known each other for a very long time. She has had other troubles, mental problems, as well as her physical illness."

"The Princess told me. I felt very sorry for Claire the other day. I hope she did not guess."

He kissed me and asked me then, "Do you pity me?"

"Good Lord, no!" Then I begged his pardon for my vehemence, but much as I loved my future husband and admired and suffered for him, it would never occur to me that there was anything pitiful about him, and I told him so.

Late that afternoon, Mother arrived with Mike and the others. It had been given out in a Court Bulletin that Prince Stefan broke his arm in a thoughtless testing of a new Cortot racing car, and no one found it odd that he suffered some pain in that arm, so the evening's festivities, though curtailed, went off very well.

Mother was so impressed by the display of wedding presents from friends, acquaintances and governments all over the world, that she could speak of nothing else, though she kept asking to see my perfect if unspectacular engagement ring, whose stone she thought too small.

"Her Highness tells me the sapphires and the diamond parure are heirlooms from some tsar or king or something."

"Some tsarina or queen or something," I corrected her, smiling at the fascination such things still held for her, although she had long ago sold the nearly three million dollars worth of jewelry she had taken along with her divorce settlement from father. I remember how careful Aunt Grace was to see that I never wore too much expensive jewelry until I was grown. She was always afraid of Mother's example. By the time I had grown up, and could wear the famous jewels of the family, I found that a pair of exquisite diamond eardrops perfectly suited almost everything I wore, and upon grand occasions, even the heavy, Amberley Emeralds did not give me quite the elegance I felt when I wore my simple necklace of matching and wonderfully faceted blue diamonds.

I thought of all Stefan's and my wedding presents and did not say what I was feeling, that I would trade them all away a million times, just for the assurance that Stefan would have a few years of freedom from accidents.

In the middle of the after-dinner liqueurs and conversation, Luc came to wish the Prince well, and I was called out to join the two men in one of the Princess' small salons. Stefan made a little possessive gesture to me that I loved and I went to him at once. Both men were very serious.

"I am afraid Luc cannot remain in Feldenstein to attend the wedding," Stefan told me as I looked from him to Luc, wondering.

"I am taking Claire back to France," Luc explained in his low, almost expressionless voice. "She died this afternoon."

I had known her condition, understood the nature of that shadowy presence I felt when I was with her, and yet, the chill that came over me at Luc's flat statement was something I was not prepared for. Even at the end, life was cruel and unjust to Claire Sebastiani. No wonder she was cruel to others. Who knew what the real Claire had been like, the child born with the optimism and dreams and high hopes most children had known at some time or other?

"She wanted to be very rich," I murmured, feeling the familiar descent of that black depression I had known several times in my life. "She was promised she could live the way she wanted to. It isn't fair. It's wrong!" As Luc looked at me oddly, I felt the inadequacy of anything I might say. "I'm so sorry. So very sorry."

I was deeply aware of Stefan's presence so close beside me, giving me the emotional strength I needed, just as he needed me physically, and I felt guiltily aware of my own luck. Stefan and Luc exchanged a few words about future plans, about meeting at Monza for the Grand Prix, and then we watched Luc leave us.

"I have you to thank for saving my life," Stefan reminded him at the last, and I added as I gave Luc my free hand and felt the hard, lean fingers close for the last time over mine, "I am the one who owes you so much, Luc, but most of all, for giving me my husband, alive and well."

Luc did not look back. We went to the terrace and watched him far below in the dark courtyard as he got into the Cortot Claire and roared away toward the highway and the Sanitorium. I moved closer to the warmth of Stefan as the night finally shrouded Luc from our sight.

I never saw Luc Sebastiani again.